This was punish... not a fight

He felt the hard, icy press of Turenne's boot on the back of his neck. He could not have resisted it—and perhaps he didn't want to. My God, my God, he cried mentally, what have I been in this life? What must I do to pay this back?

As if he had heard him, Turenne said, "You can give me something that might atone a little. There is something you can do for me."

"Name it, sir, please," Dan whispered.

"You know of the German retaliations against the Maquis, the Resistance fighters? They oftentimes shoot ten innocent people in retaliation for one Boche death. You know of this?" He took his boot off Samson's head.

Dan nodded, pushing himself up onto his hands a little and drawing a sweet lungful of clean air.

"That is my price. Give me ten dead Boche by dawn, and I may begin to think of you as human."

John Barnes

TIMERAIDER

WARTIDE

A GOLD EAGLE BOOK FROM
WORLDWIDE.

TORONTO • NEW YORK • LONDON
AMSTERDAM • PARIS • SYDNEY • HAMBURG
STOCKHOLM • ATHENS • TOKYO • MILAN
MADRID • WARSAW • BUDAPEST • AUCKLAND

First edition April 1992

ISBN 0-373-63604-0

Special thanks and acknowledgment to
John Barnes for his contribution to this work.

WARTIDE

WARTIDE

1

Matt Perney's foot came out of nowhere in a savage slap at the side of Dan Samson's head. Barely ducking in time, Samson struck back with a low, hard right cross, stepping inside Perney's striking radius to drive the blow home into Perney's exposed rib cage.

But Perney was just as fast. A hard block deflected Dan's fist so that he barely grazed Perney's side, and before he could withdraw, his wrist was caught and yanked forward. Then the sole of Perney's foot was propped against the front of Samson's ankle, and suddenly Samson was tumbling forward in a plunging somersault.

His head tucked automatically, and Samson's shoulder hit an instant later. His feet whipped over his head, and he twisted to land on his feet in a low crouch. Perney's foot was there again, striking at his face as the smaller man leaped at him.

Swiftly, Dan Samson extended his left leg, letting himself sink to the floor and moving his head back out of the path of the kick. The sole of his foot caught the back of Perney's ankle as it planted, and both his hands grabbed under Perney's belt to throw him up, away and back. As Samson fell back, he turned again, whirling in on the side so that Perney was unable to block with his legs, and dived onto his opponent.

Perney's hands came up instantly to block, but he was on his back and Samson now had the advantage. Samson could smell the copper tang of Perney's sweat and hear him breathing, a deep gasping sound, for they had been fighting for a long time. Smoothly Samson worked his hands up the lapels of Perney's jacket, tucking his head to avoid a blow or grip, and suddenly was in under Perney's collar. His thumbs gripped Perney's collar, his little fingers met behind Perney's neck, and he twisted his crossed hands to apply the knife edge of each hand against Perney's carotid and windpipe, bearing down firmly.

There was an eruption of thrashing as Perney tried to kick, twist or wriggle free, but Samson was too strong for him and moved forward so that all of his 235 pounds was bearing down on Perney's neck. Perney's face turned purple, and sweat stood out on his brow as he thrashed and kicked, then his body relaxed. . . .

He tapped Dan Samson twice on the shoulder, the quick, light acknowledgment that Dan had won. Samson released him, and they both sat up laughing. "Good round," Matt said at last.

"Whoa. Yeah. What's that make it, lifetime?"

"Freestyle or everything?"

"Either way."

Matt wiped his forehead with his sleeve. "Freestyle, you've won 849 to my 823. Total, counting boxing, judo, freestyle, *shotokan,* tae kwon do, *rinjutsu,* savate, saber, *bo-ken* and pugil sticks, I'm ahead 2022 to 2003. You obviously have trouble staying inside the rules, Dan.''

From anyone else, that would have hurt, but from his oldest and best friend it was merely the truth. Dan grinned back at him. "Only when the rules are crooked, buddy.''

Matt seemed to hold his gaze just a moment too long, as if the comment had been a little calculated, or perhaps as if he himself had just realized the implications. "God, I'm sorry about the whole deal with you getting fired," he said. "You had a lot of hopes for the job, too. Now that you've got some frustration worked out, you want to talk about it a little?''

"Maybe I do," Dan admitted. "But let's get over to a corner of the mat—sitting out here in the middle and talking sets a bad example for the kids, if any of them turn up early.''

The two friends moved to the wooden bench where parents usually sat and watched their offspring trying to brain or squash each other. Dan's eye ran over the paneled back wall of Matt's dojo—technically the Perney Academy of the Combat Arts—and came to rest quietly on the American flag, then on the calm faces of a dozen or so of the great martial-arts masters, the old black-and-white photographs kept carefully free of dust. At last his gaze stopped on three old color photos, the colors now changing oddly as the cheap dyes used in the 1960s faded, of three young men in uniforms. These days probably only he and Matt could identify who they were or what they had done, but somehow no one ever asked, perhaps because they had heard too many stories from too many Vietnam vets, or because they sensed somehow that those photographs were not subjects for casual conversation.

"So," Matt said, "what happened?"

"Thanks for not saying 'this time,'" Dan said, smiling sourly. "I should have realized that Honest John wasn't going to keep me for long. Mostly I think I was just good for publicity. Hey, let me just mention—I really appreciate you setting me up to teach here so fast— I really needed to make the rent."

"Never a problem. You're the best instructor I've got, especially with the kids. Always glad to have you. But I'm damned sorry I can't pay you much above minimum wage. Now, come on, out with it—what did our slimy friend, Honest John, ask you to do? Kidnap old ladies from church and sell them for medical experiments?"

Dan snorted. "He wouldn't do that. There's obviously no market for it since his mother's still around." With a sigh he launched into the painful story.

Honest John was John Childers, who owned a dozen large used-car lots. A few weeks before, when the Vietnam veterans memorial downtown had been dedicated, Dan had been pleasantly surprised to find that his uniform still fit and that his medals had not gotten lost in his many moves. Honest John had managed to turn the dedication ceremony into a free commercial by announcing that he was hiring fifteen new salesmen with a Viet vets hiring preference. At the time Dan had been desperate, so he'd taken the job despite his irritation.

For three weeks it had worked out pretty well, because Honest John's really did have fairly decent prices on cars, and Dan had been working in the lot down toward the Laval-Petain neighborhood, where people just needed to get basic transportation without breaking themselves financially to do it. He'd really enjoyed helping people find something that was in their range and working out a deal that seemed to be fair to everyone. Maybe because people sensed that, he beat the sales records for that lot in two of the three weeks he worked there.

Unfortunately that led to a promotion. Honest John decided he needed someone to help move new cars on the flagship lot. That wasn't nearly as much fun, because the people he was selling to just didn't need a good deal as much, and in fact what they really seemed to want was a lot of flattery and sucking up from the salesman, but he did all right until the day a guy wanted to buy the Blue Dog.

The Blue Dog was a funny shade of metallic blue, and had been ordered six months before by a customer who had disappeared after placing the order. There was nothing really wrong with it except that it had spent a long time sitting on the lot getting crudded up, but no one had been able to sell it, even though twice people had come in and ordered identical new cars.

Dan went into the manager's office to see what price he was supposed to get for the Blue Dog, and Childers had been in there with the manager.

"Dan boy, that's great! What have you told him?"

"Just that it's for sale. He wants to know the price. I think he's in love with that car, and if we don't jack this up enough to scare him, he'll drive away in it."

Childers leaned way back, stretched exultantly and said, "Oooh, Danny, today we all get rich. Tommy, when was the last time we sold a clone of the Blue Dog?"

"Three months ago," the manager said. "You want the invoice on that one?"

"You bet we do." Childers was grinning. Tom went to get it. "Now, Dan boy, you're going to see how we make real money in this game. See, what we do is you go out there with that nice big honest smile of yours and you tell him you've got the invoice on it—I know I told you guys to sell from list, but this is even better. Tell him you have to take a minimum three percent markup, but that you really want to get the thing off the lot. He'll close then and there."

"But that's not the invoice for the same car," Dan said, feeling a little bit stupid.

"Exactly, exactly!" Childers grinned at him. "Follow me through this. Maybe he knows, and if he doesn't, you make sure he realizes that an invoice is what *we* pay for the car. List is bullshit, right? So now he's getting the straight shit, and yeah, we're even telling him the truth about the minimum profit here. So he feels real warm and cozy. Hell, we're even letting the poor dork know the truth—it's a car we really want to sell and get off the lot.

"But between the time we got that first car and the time we moved this last clone of it, the manufacturer jacked prices a few times. Like it adds up to about twenty percent. So after all these months we're going to make a profit on that old dog that will make your head spin.

"And of course, if he's really smart enough to notice the date of manufacture on the invoice and compare it with the date on the door, so he catches us—we just say oopsie, honest mistake. Then he does get an honest deal, but we still get rid of the Blue Dog.

"But these guys are too dumb to think of something like that. One he thinks he's getting a bargain, he's not going to have one thought in hell that maybe it's more than he should be paying, so he gets the car he wants, the fucking Blue Dog is off my lot, and Dan-o Samson gets a whacking fat commission." The big man leaned back again, slid his hands under his ample paunch and seemed to be straightening his underwear through his Brooks Brothers pin-striped trousers.

"Couldn't I just try to get him for list? That's still like four percent profit. I'm sure he can afford it either way, but as long as he's already doing us a favor, why don't we—"

Childers didn't stop smiling anywhere except his eyes, but those drilled straight into Dan. "I sure hope you aren't going soft on me. Because I really can't use a salesman that's soft. Your job is to get these people separated from their money. If there was a way to do that without them getting any car at all, I'd be happy to."

Dan cleared his throat, trying to think of what to say. "It's just that...well, that really isn't the invoice for the car he's buying. It's sort of taking advantage of him, and I just don't feel like—"

Childers leaned forward, staring straight at Dan. "You and me need to have a little talk here," he said. "Tommy, go close on it." His arm stabbed out like a sharp, underhanded punch, thrusting the invoice at Tom. Silently, without looking at Dan, Tom got up and went off to make the sale to Dan's customer.

"No, you listen here. I don't know what kind of place you got to be weird this way—maybe you stayed awake too often in basic training or something? But I'm going to fill you in here, because I really do like you, Danny kid. It's a rough world out there, and right now, in that chair, you have got to make up your mind whether you're going to spend the rest of your life off on this truth-justice-and-the-American-way crusade or get off your lazy butt and go skin some people."

The big dealer got up and walked to the window, looking out over the vast empire of his lot full of new cars. "You know what makes this country the kind of great place it is, Dan boy? It's not those flags flying out there—" he pointed at the row of twenty American flags flying from masts at the front of Honest John's "—and it's not the nice parades once a year where guys like you get to walk up the street in your uniforms. No sir. What makes this country great is these!"

He pulled a roll of bills from his vest pocket and shook them in Dan's face. "You understand me? Right now you have to start pulling your weight and chasing some money. Or you can be a fucking loser—and this country has no regard for a loser. That's another thing that makes it great."

Dan realized that his employer was expecting him to say something. "I'm really sorry," was all he could think of. That bothered him, though, because it had been a lie, so he added, "I just can't see taking someone's money because he doesn't notice one little—"

Childers's voice snapped at him. "What I was going to say is, not like some guy that goes off and gets shot at and uses it as an excuse for twenty years. Not like some guy that expects to just make money at a job, or to have somebody fucking *give* him a job, because he's got a bunch of medals. Now I want to see a total change of attitude—"

Something simply flipped over in Daniel Samson right then. He stood up—at six-three and 235, all muscle, that was always a way to get attention—and said, "Mr. Childers, I just would like to suggest something here. I think it would improve our relationship."

Childers glared at him and said, "I'm open to your suggestion."

"My suggestion," Dan said, "is that you get out from between me and the door, so that when I leave, like I'm going to do right now, I don't knock you on your fat ass."

So Dan had left, and that had been it, except that he was out of work and broke, and Childers had even stung him for all the unpaid commissions on top of it all. He didn't see what else he could have done, but there was just one thing Childers had been right about—doing this kind of thing wasn't going to make him rich.

As he finished telling the story, he was a bit disconcerted to notice that Matt was laughing. "What?" Dan asked.

"Just the thought, buddy, that if you had knocked him flat, every Vietnam vet in the city would have been happy to kick in for a defense fund. After what he did at the memorial service…well, it's a crying shame that guys like that can wrap themselves in the flag and their money while guys like us have to work, *no, compadre?*"

Dan shrugged. "I'd like to have work as a regular thing. And you've got this place, at least."

"Gets kind of dull, pal. Not like where we've been or what we've done."

Dan grunted. "True. Easy to get out of shape and tired nowadays, isn't it? Especially when—heeeeeeeee-aiiiiii!"

He pounced on his friend ferociously. Their personal rules for "freestyle" allowed either to begin with a surprise attack, although, in their complicated scoring system, the surprise attacker had to win by more points to even up the advantage.

Matt's hands were on his lapels, and his foot came up against Samson's hipbone instantly, and they rolled over, hurling Samson onto the mat in the *tomoe-nage,* or, as nearly everyone called it after the old movies, the Apache Rifle Throw. Dan flew headfirst and tucked and rolled, then came up to face Matt's counterattack with a blur of fast punches.

None of them landed solidly, as Matt blocked rapidly, but it slowed his opponent down just enough so that Dan could try a foot sweep. Perney's foot flew out from under him, and any normal person would have fallen down, but Matt's speed and experience let him recover his balance almost instantly.

In the brief interval Dan slipped in a square, solid blow to the midsection. Matt grunted and struck back, almost succesfully jabbing Dan in the jaw, then pivoted and brought his foot up in a strike.

Dan parried the foot to the outside with his own, letting loose another whoop as he did it, and then leaped forward to close the gap between them. Matt struck again, but now he was too close to land a solid blow, and Dan's hands flew up toward his throat, an instant ahead of Matt's block. Once again Samson's hands swept up and under the collar, crossed to form a swift, soft, deadly butterfly, and slipped the stranglehold onto his friend. Once again Matt struggled, realized it was futile, and tapped out.

"Got me again, buddy. You've been practicing," Matt said.

"Just here."

"No kidding? That's funny." The dojo owner straightened his *gi* and rotated his neck once. "Seems as if you've been getting steadily faster and better for the last few months. Almost as if you felt somewhere in the back of your mind that a really big fight was coming up, and you'd gone into training for it."

"No big fight I know about, except with the Veterans Administration. And I kind of lost that one."

"That's right!" Matt's eyes widened. "You had that appointment this morning! How did it go? Not good?"

"Not good," Dan agreed. "They say it's not Post-Traumatic Stress Disorder because even though I *live* like I have it, I don't have any of the symptoms I'm supposed to—nightmares, flashbacks, attacks of irrational aggression...."

Matt roared with laughter. "You should've brought them by here sometime when we were free-sparring. Now *that's* irrational aggression."

Dan laughed, too, and then said, "So, believe it or not, they're selling me for medical experiments."

Matt gaped, and Dan hastened to explain. "You remember Charlie Young down at the VA hospital? He's got some friend, Dr. Planyard, over at the state university, who apparently wants to scan the brains of people like me."

"I've often thought somebody should," Matt said, grinning at him. "We'd better get down to the locker room and change to clean outfits. So they're going to pay to scan your brain?"

"Two hundred bucks. Of course, for that they get to do both hemispheres."

"What are they scanning for? Do they think you have a tumor or something?" Matt asked, more seriously, as they went down into the little basement locker room.

"No." Dan was a little surprised to discover that he was embarrassed to talk about this in front of such an old, close friend, but there was no getting around it now that he had mentioned it. "Uh, believe it or not, it's not that kind of scan. It's some new thing that Dr. Planyard has that brings out buried memories, really deeply buried memories."

"Like what happened when you were three, or maybe something you blocked out from Nam?" Matt turned the showers on, hot and stinging, and the two got in and lathered up.

"Hmm. Well, yeah, they bring that stuff back, but that's not what they mean by 'deep.'" Dan turned to let the heat and the force of the shower relax his back and neck muscles. He knew that at his age he was supposed to be getting sore and stiff, but he'd stayed in good enough shape that he could still take on most twenty-year-olds. Still, after a hard workout like the one he and Matt had had, this felt wonderful. He wondered if that was the first sign of old age.

"So what's deeper than that? Memories from the womb?"

"Before that, actually," Dan said.

"You don't mean...past-life bullshit, do you? I'm not going to see you on *Geraldo* or something?"

Samson laughed. "God, I hope not. No, Charlie says they don't really know what to make of it. They set it for middle depth and they get all that stuff a shrink would get out of you on the couch, so it's a great tool— except that they're trying to figure out why there's a few people with memories so deep that they can hardly get to the bottom. And why a lot of it really does look like 'past-life' stuff. Charlie says it doesn't mean that I'm reincarnated or anything—though it doesn't mean I'm *not,* if you see what I mean. It could just be some strange thing the mind does, using up a lot of memory space on some kind of vivid hallucinations."

Matt shrugged. "So how do they know you have them?"

"They don't, but I fit the profile, and they're willing to pay two hundred bucks to find out. Really, buddy, they just stick some wires into my head—no trouble at all. And I need the cash."

Matt killed the showers and threw him a towel from the warmer. "Yeah, well, something about it gives me a not-good feeling. But like you say, you need the cash. Just promise me you'll cut and run if it looks even a little weird."

"When have I ever run away from something weird?"

Matt snapped his towel at him, but it was distinctly halfhearted. "Don't know why, but I really do have a bad feeling about it. You be careful."

"You going to be on *Geraldo* as a psychic the week after I'm on with my past lives?"

His friend smiled. "Maybe. What does Sarah think of all this?"

Dan fell silent for a moment as he thought of his ex-wife, her red hair gleaming in the sunlight, her green eyes sparkling behind her granny glasses. He looked away and shrugged, but a smile tugged at the corners of his mouth. "Well, you know Sarah. She likes the idea. She always had a weakness for New Age stuff, so this is right up her alley."

"You two seem to be getting along better since the divorce."

"Well, it's a lot easier to be old friends than it was to be married."

"Glad to hear it." Matt brightened up and slapped Dan on the shoulder. "Let's get dressed. We're going to have some help with the kid class today."

"Help?"

"You remember our old master, Jei Yul Kim?"

"No," Dan said, laughing. "I've completely forgotten the little guy who used to scream at us in six languages, trying to make us learn to keep our balance low and not look at our feet. And I don't remember anything about having to take down an eight-inch tree with our bare hands in ten minutes to graduate."

Matt laughed, too, the easy laugh of an old friend, and threw an arm around Dan. "Okay, so you got all the sense of humor. It's a good thing I got all the charm and good looks. Yeah, that was a dumb question. Well, I got a letter from Master Kim today."

"Wow! I hadn't heard from him in twenty years."

Matt explained, "The other thing is, it didn't exactly come by mail. It was a letter of introduction."

"He sent someone to us?"

"He did. A Master Xi, who will be here as a guest teacher for a week. The thing I found most interesting is that he also said specifically—and this was strange, because he had no way of knowing that the two of us were even in touch with each other—that he really wanted you to meet Master Xi."

"Huh. Well, great, I'm really looking forward to it."

There was a polite cough at the doorway. An old, white-haired Oriental stood there. His face, lined with great age, was perfectly calm, and his carriage was still erect. He was tall, maybe taller than Samson himself, and though no bulges of muscles showed through the

canvas jacket and trousers of his *gi,* there was a strength
about him that suggested he could do almost anything.

"I am in the presence of Daniel Samson?" the older
man said.

"Yes, sir," Dan said, bowing.

The old master bowed deeply himself and then
smiled. "Jei Yul Kim was most emphatic that I should
seek you out. I'm glad to have found you. I understand, however, that we will have many children in here
in a very short time, so I suppose conversation must
come later."

He had no sooner spoken then the door banged and
the Russell twins roared downstairs into the locker
room, bickering and squabbling, to dress for class.

"Parent-teacher days," Matt said. "They all love me
for opening the dojo and giving the kids a place to be.
But the little guys are always so wild after spending the
day tearing up the house, I'm not sure I'm doing much
more than baby-sitting."

"They're good kids," Dan said. "Just a little extra
energy."

"They've got that," Matt agreed. "I really appreciate your coming in to take the special class—and for the
workout."

The front door thumped another three times, and
more kids poured into the locker room, shouting excitedly to one another.

Matt, Dan and Master Xi went into Matt's office to
finish talking and to leave more room for the kids.

"What do you think these children especially need to work on?" Master Xi asked Dan. "I believe I can help you with many things—which would you prefer?"

It was on the tip of Dan's tongue to say that they needed to work on foot techniques, both sweeps and kicks, because so many small kids have trouble balancing on one foot, when a thought struck him and he just blurted out, "You know, there's all sorts of technique things we could work on, but I really feel that the big problem with today's kids is fighting spirit. They give up too easily. It's like they make one effort to show you they're trying, and then, blooey, they just hang back and lose. Even the really aggressive ones, who will beat the daylights out of a kid smaller or weaker or not as eager as they are—if they aren't winning, they give up."

"This *is* serious," Master Xi said. "I have seen it many times. Perhaps we can find something we can do for them."

"Hi, Dan." When Samson turned, the tiny boy standing in the doorway seemed to be all big dark eyes and huge hands and feet.

"Hey, Tony. Here to kill today?"

The little boy's hand had gone to his mouth—Dan suspected he was having trouble not sucking his thumb—and he shrugged and nodded, but he didn't show much enthusiasm.

"Better get dressed, we'll be starting soon."

Tony scampered into the locker room. "He really likes you," Matt said. "I think you're the only reason he keeps coming. But boy, he sure gets clobbered—even though in standing practice his form is the best in the class."

Master Xi nodded as if he had heard something profound. "Was it this child you were thinking of, Mr. Samson?"

"Uh-huh. To some extent. But all of them, too."

The kids were filing into the mat room now, and it really didn't do to let them have time to get wild, so Dan went in to line them up. He set them a brisk warm-up—at least he had gotten the kids to stop cheating on push-ups and sit-ups in the past couple of months. He didn't know whether to blame their parents or the TV, but it had been a real battle.

When they were all warmed up and sweating a little—and not incidentally, didn't have quite so much energy to cut up with—Dan introduced Master Xi and turned the class over to him.

"Today," Master Xi said, "we are going to study fear. Fear is the thing that so often keeps us from what we should be, what we could be. And yet, fear is nothing at all."

He looked around the room again and said quietly, "Let me repeat that. Fear is nothing at all. Fear is a natural, ordinary thing for you to feel, and if you stay at this as long as I have—and I am, as you have no doubt noticed, quite an old man—you will still feel fear every time you face an opponent.

"It is natural to feel fear when you are in danger of being hurt. It is natural, for that matter, to have a runny nose when you have a cold. But you can work with a runny nose and you can fight while you are afraid. That is really all there is to it.

"Do we have blindfolds, Mr. Samson?"

"Yes, sir." Dan went and got them. He could hear Xi repeating his theme to the kids. At least they were all being quiet, standing still, not embarrassing Matt or the dojo.

"Have you all learned *chugari,* the somersault fall?" The class nodded doubtfully.

"Mr. Samson, please blindfold me and lead me to a corner of the mat." Dan did. "Now please bend, with your hands on your knees, at the very center of the mat."

Dan gripped his knees, knowing what was coming—Master Kim had done this, years ago. He watched the kids' faces. Master Xi, surprisingly lithe and agile, raced across the mat toward Dan. Blindfolded though he was, at the last instant he shot straight up into the air, clearing Dan's bent back by a foot, and came down headfirst, catching himself in a clean roll and rising to his feet.

"I will tell you one secret. I counted how many of my steps it took to get to the center of the mat. Naturally, running and jumping so hard, I knew I could be hurt and I felt fear. But because, coming back, I counted my steps, I simply paid all my attention to that, and none to my fear—and though I was afraid, I did it." He looked around the room. "Now each of you, count your steps. You are all going to do this."

Solemnly—when had Dan ever seen them so well behaved?—they counted off the steps from the center to the corner. Then, one at a time Dan blindfolded each of them, and they ran to vault over Master Xi, who was bent low. The first up was one of the Russells—no one could tell them apart—and after he went over, Master Xi himself removed the blindfold and said, "Were you afraid?"

"No, that was fun."

"Then you were not paying attention. Do it again. This time, before you start, think about what will happen if you miss. Face it. See that you could trip, you could fall, you could land on your face or twist an ankle or wrist. Do you understand?"

"Y-yes." The boy looked more nervous than Dan would ever have thought possible. "Now go back, have Mr. Samson blindfold you, and let's try again."

This time the boy wavered a moment before beginning, and Master Xi shouted, "Count your steps and go!"

He did.

"Did you feel fear this time?"

"Yes, I did." There was something else there, a new confidence, something Dan had not heard before.

"You see, a man who does not feel fear is merely a fool. A man who does not know he is in danger cannot be brave. Courage is to know you are afraid, and why you are afraid, and to do it anyway. As long as you rely on not thinking, on not knowing, the first little bit of imagination can paralyze you with terror. And you will come to trust everything to your own foolishness and will never be able to look reality in the eye, or worse still, you will become a coward. Fear must be your best friend and your brother, and must walk beside you every day of your life." He gave the Russell kid a light hug and said, "Fear is a good companion, warning you of danger, keeping you from stupidity, but he is a poor master. Keep him with you, but rule him."

The boy, his eyes huge, nodded, and Dan realized that this was going to stay with the Russell kid forever. Well, it might do him some good, and it was certainly more valuable than half the crap they taught in school.

Out of the corner of his eye, Dan had seen little Tony maneuver to the back of the line, and as Master Xi worked his way down the row of students—sometimes making one go back and face the fear, sometimes praising an unusually quick or graceful student, always patiently keeping them trying until they did well—Tony seemed to withdraw into himself more and more. Dan knew this was going to be a problem, and worse yet, it would be happening in front of all the other kids. His heart bled for Tony, but he really didn't see what he could do.

At last it was the tiny boy's turn. Tony started and stopped, started and stopped, and then Master Xi very gently said, "This is good. You are meeting fear thoroughly. Now that you know him, you know that even though he is very big, he is only so big, and no bigger. Now, count your steps, and go!"

Tony charged forward, and his little voice screamed out, "One, two, three..." as he came. With a huge, high vault, he sailed far over Master Xi and landed in a beautiful *chugari,* coming straight back up to attention and standing quietly.

Master Xi knelt and gently unblindfolded the boy. "Something was very hard for you, but you faced it anyway," he said. The room was so quiet they could have heard a fly alight or a creak of the floorboard. Everyone, Dan included, seemed to be holding his breath. "Tell me what this thing that was so difficult was."

Tony looked up solemnly into Master Xi's face and said, "I forgot how many steps it was."

Master Xi gave a great, glad shout of laughter and whirled the boy up over his head. "That is best of all! That is superb! You forgot a detail that made no difference, for all you really needed to do was to get over my back, and you faced fear without any crutch at all! This is very good!"

He set him down, sent him to the line and said, "And now I think I should like to see you all spar."

That kept Dan busy for the rest of the session. He always had to keep a careful eye on them to make sure no one was cheating, that punches and kicks continued to be pulled, to shout encouragement to children who hung back and dampen the enthusiasm of anyone who started to really hit in earnest. Master Xi and Matt also moved around the room, encouraging, praising, correcting, helping, but the three adults were far too busy to talk to each other. So it was only just before the end of class that Dan happened to look over and see Tony cornering and subduing a boy twice his size.

When class was dismissed, Dan noticed that they were all quiet and straight in line, and he realized that they had something that they hadn't had before—dignity.

As he was changing in the locker room, Master Xi came in to talk to him. "Master Kim was right, I think. There is a shadow I can see behind you, but it is not fear, not the common shadow."

Dan nodded politely, not sure where this was going, as he buttoned his shirt.

"There is something, Daniel Samson, that you need to be doing, something that you are not doing now, and a part of you seems to know what it is. I do not think you are avoiding it—I think you merely have not been able to see what it is as yet."

Dan was going to ask more, but then he saw his watch. "Oh, I'm sorry, sir, but there's something I should be doing in fifteen minutes and it's two miles away! I really have to get moving! But if you'll be here for the week, I'm sure I will be able to talk to you again—"

"Oh, yes, we'll talk again. And I quite agree that you don't want to be late for something so important." Master Xi smiled at him and added, "I look forward to the many times I am sure we will see each other."

With a wave to Matt, Dan was out the door and running toward the university. It was a good thing it was all slightly downhill because after three hours of sparring with Matt, and the moderate workout you always got teaching class, it was pleasant to be able to run without much effort.

Well, he'd always stayed in shape. That twenty-year-old uniform still fit him as though it had been tailored.

In fact, he thought, it was kind of strange, but if they'd take him at his age, he could probably do just fine going back into the Army. Maybe even still Special Forces. Between the dojo and other working out—and, let's see, it had been how many years that he'd been getting his deer on the first day of the season? Anyway, several. He might have to learn to use a new weapon or two....

Unfortunately there'd have to be a pretty major war before a man in his midforties would be wanted. Cannon fodder was definitely a young man's game.

2

He had no trouble finding the lab on the third floor of the psych building, right where Charlie Young had said it would be. He was quickly ushered into the back office to meet a tall, bald, thin man with thick glasses. "Dr. Planyard?"

"Solly, please. And you must be Dan Samson. Charlie Young had your records sent over, so I know pretty much everything I need. If you like, we can put you under, I can get the recording, give you your two hundred, and then whatever other information I need, I can phone you for after I get back from this trip."

"I appreciate your trusting me—"

"Anyone Charlie will vouch for is no gamble. You look like you're sweating—did you just exercise? The equipment's downstairs here." They went downstairs together, Planyard waving at his secretary on the way out.

"Uh, yeah, I did have a fairly heavy workout today, actually...."

"It's no problem. To some extent it seems to help the pseudomemory recovery, so if anything, this is better. Okay, this room here."

Dan's first thought, on seeing the apparatus, was that it really looked a lot like an old-fashioned electric chair.

"Looks like something I'd use to get rid of uncooperative students, doesn't it? But those things that go around your wrists and ankles read muscle tension—they don't hold you in—and the part for your chest is pretty much the same thing you'd find on a lie detector. And as for what's in the silly metal hat, I'd love to talk about that, but we don't have all day, and ever since universities learned about the benefits of patents, none of us has been allowed to talk about anything, anyway." Planyard helped Dan into the chair and made sure he was comfortable. "If you need to take a leak, say so now, because you're going to be in this thing an hour and a half."

"No, I'm fine."

"Okay. It's really very easy for you. I'll dim the lights and put on some soothing noise.... You like folk music?"

"It's all right."

"Good, because it's what I have. You just sit and try to be calm. You probably won't be able to fall asleep, but if you do, that's okay. You will find yourself having what you might experience either as very vivid dreams or as memories. Don't let them worry you much, and you needn't try to remember them. The part I'm interested in, which is the brain waves, is getting recorded.

"The one safety precaution is this—whatever happens, unless the building is on fire or something, *don't* get out of the chair until the session is done. Not that it would really hurt you, but after we do all the pseudo-memory recovery, we put a very mild suppressor wave back into the process so that when you get up you won't be overwhelmed by all those new memories. You could be pretty severely disoriented for a few hours if you left early. That's also why you need to stay in the chair and you can't, for example, go down the hall to the bathroom.

"But even if we had a power failure or something in the middle, you'd be just fine in two or three hours. Any questions?"

Dan couldn't think of any, so the lights came down, Solly Planyard left the room, and Peter, Paul, and Mary started coming through the speakers. Well, this was certainly light work . . . and it seemed pretty tough for Dan to screw it up or get fired.

He felt drowsy, but not really ready to go to sleep. He seemed to feel things moving in his brain, memories of being called by other names, running to his mother, but she looked different, at a tiny log cabin somewhere up in the mountains, the blaze of desert sunlight, *frantically working to clear a jammed gun—water in the jacket frozen!—subzero weather—the Boche pouring out of their trenches, trying to see through the fogged lens of his gas mask—*

Well, Planyard had told him the truth. This certainly was vivid. He guessed it must be unusually vivid, because he heard Planyard's low whistle outside the door and some assistant talking excitedly.

A French knight bearing down on him, Dan—no, Jock, but who's Jock?—stepping sideways, his pike blade batting the lance tip to the side as he grounded his pike and leveled it into the onrushing metal monster's visor—

Whew, this was quite a ride. He saw the sun rise over the Caribbean and a storm blow in across the steppes—never having been either place. They ought to be able to charge for this . . . it beat hell out of Disneyland, anyway.

The signal came and the phalanx lowered the spears and advanced—

The great bombards pitched their stone balls against the earthworks, and the shock came up through his feet—

Parthian arrows rained down as if from the hot Mesopotamian sun itself, the wagons on fire behind them, and Dan—or was it Caius?—hurled his last pilum, too short, drew his shortsword as at last they closed in. . . . Guard the back of the man in front of you, never look behind, die in your tracks but keep moving forward at the same pace as the rest of your rank just like in drill—

The chatter of an AK-47 outside, and the screams, some of fear, one of pain, and a young voice, a boy's voice, yelling "Communist fucking gooks!"

The last one was different. A lot of things like that he had heard, but no, this was—

It wasn't a memory. He was abruptly wide-awake.

Again a shot came from the hall, a crumpled thud, a shriek, and yet another shot and a voice screaming, "Communists selling the country out ... can't win with one hand tied behind our fucking back ... Jews and niggers taking over ... white girls with beaners ..."

Dan rolled out of the chair, heedless of the tearing gauges or the clang the headpiece made as it hit the floor. Everything swirled for a moment, but the adrenaline cut through, and he was through the door—Solly Planyard lying facedown in front of him, the back of his head a shredded mess. Obviously he'd looked out the door and taken a bullet.

Dan yelled, "Medic!" automatically and kept going, tossing the door wide and rolling across the hall, then pinning himself up in a door arch. A slug screamed off a fluorescent light fixture.

"I am dedicated ... I am totally the man in control here ... we are number one and we are going to stay that way and blond chicks are for white guys—"

"Tommy, please!" another voice was whispering.

Dan darted a quick look, pulled back. Another slug grazed the linoleum at his feet and smashed a window on an office somewhere. Outside someone was yelling to call 911.

Dan let the picture his brain had snapped develop. Kid, not more than twenty. About thirty feet down the hall. Had an AK-47 and a pale, scared blond girl by the hair. Brown-skinned kid on the ground, possibly dead. Girl curled in fetal position on floor a few feet up the hallway, dead or hurt bad. Unconscious boy on floor, possibly still bleeding, maybe alive?

"The fucking spirit God bless America of Vietnam lives. White people and America and God, fucking A." A couple of pointless shots blew out more office windows. "Next war we *are* the SS! We *are* the Nazis! We *are* dedicated! We kicked butt in Nam and we'll kick all the other butt there is. God bless America!"

Good thing it was late Friday afternoon, fewer victims around, Dan thought.

The picture kept developing. There was a metal cylinder ashtray, six feet away. He seemed to hear one of the instructors, a voice he hadn't thought of in ages. *Rule one of unarmed combat is don't stay unarmed. Find a weapon. A bottle, a rock, a stick, sand for the eyes, a chicken bone, a necktie, a fucking tree but find it now.*

Another voice—he didn't know from where—was whispering, *You shouldn't have gotten out of the chair. But since you did, you're here, and you can hear me, notice that kid's got a boner big as Christmas and his shirt's split from muscle tension. Eyes dilated to the max. Berserk, probably on PCP and maybe meth. Talks like a neo-Nazi, KKKer, something like that. Too young to be a combat vet, probably just likes to play with guns. No real training and probably not much practice, but with those symptoms, supernaturally strong, will feel no pain. Sounds like the girl is what he flipped about. If she's actually his girlfriend or sister, she may turn on you when you attack. Straight shit—you can't do anything but kill him. There will be more victims if you don't, and three of the people in this hall have to get to an ER in twenty minutes or less. No time for a hostage situation.*

One last, cold, thin voice whispered, *Fear is a good companion but a poor master.*

Dan whipped a handful of change from his pocket slantwise down the hall. As it crashed against the wall, he rolled out in a *chugari,* grabbing the ashtray, and came up throwing the metal top. Sand, cigarette butts and the metal top flew into the face of the young psychotic as Dan veered and rolled again, closing the distance. A slug thudded into the floor near his head, and he changed direction again as something shoved hard into his armpit.

He spun a kick, and the muzzle slapped harmlessly upward toward the ceiling, two shots spraying off, as he stepped in and chopped with his good arm, hard against the side of the neck.

His muscles are too tense to dent, Solly Planyard's voice whispered again, *the larynx, the larynx.*

Dan hit hard again, and felt the crunch of cartilage. The gun boomed impossibly loud, and as if from far away, Dan felt his thighbone shatter. In the instant, as he waited to fall, he jabbed his fingers into the foe's eyes and on the way down caught the AK in his good hand, twisted, turned.

There was another explosion, and the hand gripping his hair relaxed. It was suddenly very quiet. The voices in his head were gone, and it was very dark and getting darker. There was sobbing, and he could hear the gruff voices of cops on the stairs.

Two things always amaze everyone in a crisis—how quickly the police arrive, and then how slowly everything goes after that. The final toll seemed to be two faculty members, Solomon Planyard and Michael Hemor, and a grad assistant, Hector Angelo, dead. Nine students had been wounded, not counting the girl he had grabbed, who had a concussion but had not been shot. The psychotic attacker, blinded and with a crushed throat, was bleeding to death internally as the paramedics labored over him. . . .

The Unknown Hero, as the papers were to dub him for the several days before he was identified, the man who had fought back with his bare hands, lay on a stretcher, his pulse barely flickering. They ran blood into him, though not as fast as it poured out, and shone lights in his eyes to see if the pupils would contract.

No one seemed to see the tall Oriental who walked through the hallway. He was dignified enough to be taken for a dean and had the presence to be a high-ranking detective or even a city official, but he was none of these, and even if people looked directly at him, they never remembered him afterward.

He walked through the gawkers and the police and the medical people, till he came to the gurney on which Daniel Samson was being carried down to the waiting ambulance. One long-fingered, delicate hand reached out and touched Samson's forehead, as if to wipe away a drop of blood or an insect.

Dan Samson's body was no longer there.

Master Xi silently withdrew and walked away. No one saw him, for they were too preoccupied with the cries of bafflement and horror from the paramedics and the ambulance crew. The dying man had simply disappeared. The confusion would grow worse in a few minutes, when they realized that none of them could quite remember what the man on the gurney had even looked like, or anything about him at all—except what he had done.

Master Xi turned once, to look back at the building, and heard them all shouting. He shook his head sadly. "They worry so much about the mere common clay, when that is not him at all. But while his spirit was here with them, it could have walked right by, clothed in that flesh, and they would have seen nothing of any significance." He sighed. "When will people open their eyes? Well, at least Jei Yul Kim was right. I was needed here. And now that this one is freed for his purpose, I have other places to be."

If anyone had been watching, they would have seen Master Xi turn toward the late-afternoon sun, take a step or two, and disappear completely. But even if they had seen, they would never have recalled it afterward.

3

It was dark, and there seemed to be a great howling wind, and he blew forward in the wind, swirling and spinning. Dan had heard about near-death experiences, but this didn't seem anything like them.

Of course not, a voice said to him. *You've got a lot to do before you can die.*

There was no tone, no sound to the voice. Dan could hear nothing in the wind, and could see nothing in the darkness. But somehow he knew it was Solly Planyard. *You're dead.*

Yep. But I'm free to go over, so I'm going to. It's a good thing the equipment accidentally woke you up—that is, if there is any such thing as an accident—or there'd be a lot more of us dead. And now you're really free to do what you need to.

Dan felt fear catch at him. *What do I need to do?*

You have to find that out for yourself. But you will. I'm going over now, to the other side. I'll see you there, I'm sure I will.

Dan felt the presence of Solly Planyard grow suddenly faint, and knew that although he could move in many directions, where Solly was going, he could not follow. *Wait! How do I find out what I'm supposed to do?*

Solly's voice seemed somehow faint or distant. There was just an instant when it was very clear. *Whatever you think, if it's a question that makes sense, you'll know the answer as soon as you think it. Here nothing is hidden, if we only want to know.* And then there was no sound, no light to change, no sense of touch or motion, but Dan knew that Solly was really gone.

Well, all right. He would try anything once. *Where am I?*

An instant later he knew. *I am drifting in the Wind Between Time.*

Am I dead?

I have been. That answer didn't make much sense, but Dan had to admit he didn't know much about being dead, either.

I'd really like to just go home, he thought, and knew at once, *but what I remember isn't home. The road to real home is long and full of twists and danger, and I might just end up trapped somewhere worse than where I was trapped before, and in more danger of being lost forever.*

He felt a cold roil of fear, like an icy snake moving somewhere deep inside him, and he welcomed it, because fear was an old partner. *So, before, I was trapped in that other time? And now...*

Now the gate is open. The road is in front of me. And the chances of success are very small, and I really don't know what to do next.

Well, Dan thought to himself, *all right. Then I will just make up my mind to start and—*

It was cold.

He looked out over a rocky mountain landscape of ice and mud, and for a moment he didn't know where he was or what he was doing. Behind him there was a tiny stucco-on-earth cottage with a roof of broken tile. In front of him, down the slope, a thin, frozen creek wound its way through a ravine. Beyond that the jagged hogback ridge clawed at the low gray sky, dripping with wet snow and greasy black patches of mud.

Supposedly the winter of 1943-44 was having the worst weather that Italy had seen in twenty years, and he damned well believed it. This was like all the really bad Februaries he could remember rolled into one.

Damn, it was cold, and he wished Bronski—

It came to him. He was Jackson Houston, the private least likely ever to make private first class. The creek that wound through the ravine in front of him joined the Volturno nine miles to the west, just below Colli al Volturno. The godforsaken little village over three ridges behind them, San Benedicto, was where . . .

Holy shit.

He realized the noises behind him were created by Bronski. Yesterday, at Colli al Volturno, Jackson Houston had taken a crate of canned soup—which his own platoon did not know had arrived on the mule-train, and after three solid weeks of K rations, would have murdered him in cold blood for taking . . .

Dan's stomach rolled over. Who the hell was this Jackson Houston?

He had delivered that crate of soup to a horrible leathery old crone, who today, in turn, had delivered—bound hand and foot and gagged—her granddaughter, a girl of about fourteen to Jackson Houston. Corporal Bronski had paid extremely well for first ones on the girl, and now he was in the little abandoned farmhouse—really barely a cottage up in the wild Apennines—unwrapping his prize. After Bronski was done, if she was still in any shape for it—and from what he knew of Bronski, she might well be dead—then Jackson Houston would get seconds, and perhaps sell her to a couple other men he could trust. Or he could just untie her and let her see if she could make it back on her own.

Dan whirled and looked inside. The girl was kicking, for Bronski had cut the bonds around her ankles, but with her hands tied together and pinned behind her by both their weight, she had no chance. As Dan drew one breath and wondered if he might throw up, Bronski took a bayonet, slipped it under the girl's dress between her breasts, and slit downward.

She wore no underwear—of course not, hell, she didn't have *shoes,* and the feet that kicked at the big, brutish corporal were callused and black with dirt and old blood wherever the rags did not cover them. As the dress fell open, she was suddenly naked. Bronski seemed to freeze a moment as he looked at the white rise of her plump breasts, the straight hips not yet widened to womanhood. Despite her breasts she was just a little girl, her face streaked with tears and snot, terror and horror.

Bronski was going to hurt her the way he hurt anything weak he could get his hands on, the thought flashed into Dan's mind, and he snarled, "Bronski, you cover her and untie her right now, and I won't kill you."

"Fuck you, Jack. You ain't double-crossing me. I paid you top price to rip this little pigeon's cherry, and I'm doing it. I don't care what price you can get for her anywhere else."

He reached for her, twisting a breast so that she screamed with pain against the unyielding gag, a piercing, choked stab of suffering into Dan's ears, and Dan unslung his M-1. Shit, I've never even *seen* one of these things, he had just time to think before he realized it felt as natural in his hand as his old deer rifle.

Bronski jumped off the girl and backed up with gratifying speed. "Shit, Jack—hey, Houston, it's me, buddy, what the fuck's got into you?"

"You wouldn't believe it if I told you," Dan said truthfully. He chanced a free hand to throw a blanket over the girl. Jesus, these old M-1s were too heavy to handle one-handed! Bronski took a tenth of a step, and Dan had him back under the M-1's threatening eye. "Back up real slow, now, over into the corner, the blind corner there."

The girl was lying there, wide-eyed, not able to tell yet whether this was a rescue or merely a change of rapist.

Now that Dan had an instant to think as he watched Bronski, he realized the place stank incredibly of sheep. Up above the village—if you could call the eight occupied hovels of San Benedicto a village—like this, it had probably once been the summer quarters of a shepherd. It smelled as though he was still in business but had built a better one somewhere else and relegated this one to sheltering the animals.

Dan moved around slowly, keeping Bronski covered, and with a sudden motion turned the girl over, wishing he spoke ten words of Italian so he could tell her what was going on. Still watching Bronski, he took the commando knife that Houston had swiped from some Eighth Army limey and cut the ties on the girl's wrists and her gag.

She was up at once, for one heart-stopping instant blocking his shot at Bronski.

The flash of young pale skin must have been too much for Bronski. He took a single step, and Samson moved to cover him.

"Jesus, are you crazy?" Bronski asked. "There's a kraut patrol up here somewhere, remember, stupid? One shot and they'll be over to see what's up, and so will Flenstein and the whole platoon. I don't want to meet up with either of them, not with what we've been doing up here."

Dan said nothing.

"I don't know what your game is, but if you're not gonna be reliable in business, then you know god-damned well there's nothing left for you, 'cause you sure ain't no soldier." He fastened his pants. "I can't believe I just got stiffed. We had a deal! I can't believe you did this to me. I don't know what you paid for her, or who to, but you better hope you can get it back because I don't care what fucking happens, you're going to give me my money back."

Dan listened impassively. He realized that Bronski was more or less a rat, dangerous only when cornered or when all the advantages were on his side. All he had to do was give him a chance to slink away, and that would be the end of it. "Why don't you just head on down?"

"Yeah, why don't I fucking do that? But I haven't forgotten my money or my Luckies. No way in hell have I forgotten those. I expect to see them coming back real soon." With as much dignity as a man can muster when his underwear is literally in a bundle, Bronski hitched himself up and reached for his own M-1.

"You watch where you point that," Dan said.

"Okay, boss. Okay, whatever you say. Shit."

Holding it by the barrel, all but dragging it after him, Bronski stomped out of the little ruined cottage into the just-breaking wan February sunlight.

Immediately he fell over sideways, the side of his head bulging in a way that Dan found all too familiar.

He wasn't sure if it was himself or Jackson Houston who jumped to the wall beside the cottage's one little slit window—just a roughly rectangular hole in the thick earthen brick—and took a cautious peek.

This was a lot like the movies of Dan's youth. There were about a dozen men in German uniforms, rifles at ready, advancing slowly on Dan's position.

Well, they were bunched up, and if he—nope, no grenades. So he would set for rock and roll....

Whoever Jackson Houston had been, he was probably snickering. The M-1 was only semiauto. And these guys in the big, heavy gray coats looked as though they knew their business. He suspected the minute a rifle poked out of the this window, he'd be drawing fire.

So he did it before he had time to worry. He popped up and took a fast snap-shot, really just to make them get their heads down and slow that inevitable, Frankenstein-monster walk that their heavy boots and gear gave them, but he seemed to get a bit lucky. It looked like their pointman was at least wounded.

Dan didn't stop to take stock. He just fired as quickly as he could. They were all down on the ground now, firing back. If they'd known there was just one, they could have rushed him and had him, but until they figured that out the safe thing for them to do was to stay down.

He hit another one—a lucky shot, because a man on the ground isn't easy—and then the fire converging on the window began in earnest, German rounds spraying

fine white dust off the foot-thick sill as they shrieked to
their resting places in the back wall. He rolled over to
the door, picked his angle and popped out just in time
to see a large German with a potato-masher grenade
making the last spring to the little cottage. Dan
squeezed off a round, but as the man fell, he pitched the
grenade, and though it missed the window, several
cracks spread across the wall and a third of the roof slid
forward down the supporting members and crashed to
the ground.

Where the hell was the platoon?

There really hadn't been time for them to get here.
Well, he'd improvise. He dragged Bronski's M-1 in by
its stock, in the hope that it might save him a reload in
a second or two, and scooted to the hole just in time to
see two Germans stand up to rush.

Two more rounds put them back down, one of them
probably wounded, but they were slowly getting closer,
and as soon as one of them got in range to pitch a grenade through that fresh hole in the roof tiles, that would
be it for both him and the girl.

He popped up at the window and used the rest of the
clip to make their heads stay down. There were no real
targets, but he knew where they were, and he hoped
enough slugs would be close enough to keep them
nervous. He could hear one of them bellowing, probably a sergeant or a lieutenant, but he couldn't get a fix
on it, and the two that were still firing back were getting excessively close to the window.

He dropped to his knees, grabbed Bronski's M-1 and rolled to the doorway. He swore when he realized that the thing was jammed, and the Jackson Houston part of his memory seemed to think this was in character. An M-1 took a lot more maintenance than an M-16, and a guy like Bronski tended to forget that he was here to take part in a war.

He rolled and grabbed a spare clip and reloaded.

But Bronski's unworkable piece of rusty junk had cost him time he didn't have. A potato masher sailed right in through the window. Not even thinking, Dan flicked it out the door and lay flat as another deafening, blinding roar took out a good part of the wall on his side. With a groan, masonry began to fall forward, and he backed up under the roof, the girl now huddling beside him because there was nowhere else to be, as most of the wall fell to rubble in front of them.

The instant it was down, he wriggled forward, sighted over the top and got a good, clean shot at the officer, who had just stood up. The man went down with a cry, and that seemed to cue them all to open up, including one guy with a submachine gun. He hugged the ground and hoped they weren't coming forward.

Then he heard the pounding of three BARs, and the sharp barks of several more M-1s. The platoon was here.

He brought his M-1 up again and was pleased to see the remaining Germans hugging the ground now. The ones in the rear, including that damned submachine gun, laid down covering fire, and before the platoon could get itself properly set, they were back down the hillside. Two more Germans fell to shots from the American side, and Dan got one who didn't watch his cover, but the firefight was over as quickly as it had begun.

Now would come the long period of squirming on bellies until both sides were out of range of each other. At least the Germans would be back across that little no-name creek. That was one for the good guys. And several of them were dead, which was two. And finally, Bronski was dead, and although it wasn't officially the way he was supposed to feel, Dan sort of figured that was another one for the good guys.

A voice, heavy with a Brooklyn accent, said to him, "Pretty impressive shooting, Houston. But how'd you happen to be up here shooting at them in the first place?" It came out "inna foist place," and though Dan had never heard it before, with Jackson Houston's memories he knew it instantly.

"It looked like there was going to be trouble, so I came up," he said. It was the truth as far as it went, and Dan was a firm believer in keeping the story as close to the truth as possible. He realized it was another trait he did not share with Jackson Houston.

"First thing you've volunteered for that I ever heard about," Flenstein said.

Dan realized what strange thoughts had been ticking around in the back of his brain. Jackson Houston, with all his other charming qualities as a black marketeer, thief, liar and coward, had also been a thoroughgoing bigot, and his lieutenant's accent had bothered him because, he realized, he hated getting orders from a Jew.

So far as Daniel Samson could tell, the only things that Jackson Houston had ever done right seemed to amount to being a fairly good shot and having taken care of his weapon.

More interestingly, Dan wondered, since he had Jackson Houston's memories, apparently in perfect detail, did he have his body?

"Are you okay, Houston? You look dazed."

"Thinking, sir."

"I imagine. Well, let's start the crawl back. The sun's going down and that was a small unit, so they won't be looking for us."

They bundled Bronski up in burlap sacking—not as antiseptic as the body bags Dan remembered—and slung him over the back of a mule to be handed over to the mule train from the east side that was to meet them in three days. No one seemed to have any very strong opinions about it. It was as if he had not existed. And no one talked to Dan.

A runner had been sent over to San Benedicto, and within a few minutes a couple of soldiers were escorting the dazed girl, wrapped in a blanket, back down the hill.

Daniel Samson realized, from his Jackson Houston memories, that very few men in the unit would have missed him if he had died with Bronski.

He wasn't sure what he had jumped into, but just at the moment he passionately wished he could jump back out. Especially as he tackled the K rations, as the only man in the unit who knew there could have been something better...and who could he tell?

4

After dinner he was summoned to the lieutenant's HQ, a pup tent. The summons was delivered by a huge goon of a man named Scott, who very obviously did not like Jackson Houston.

Hell, Dan thought as they walked up to the tent, he himself didn't like Jackson Houston one bit. The man's whole career was that of social scum, a petty criminal caught in the draft who had simply used the war to become a bigger criminal.

Worse yet, nothing had forced him to be worthless. An expert shot, physically hardy, he could have been a first-rate soldier, if he had just ... well, if he had just been like Dan Samson.

The shaving mirror in his kit—not that anyone shaved out here!—revealed that Private Jack Houston had the same face as Dan Samson, and since no one was having any trouble recognizing him, he would just have to accept that as a given. Anyway, he was here now, there was a war on and in such a situation he knew what to do.

He just wished he didn't have to live down this clown's whole previous life.

Sergeant Scott lifted the tent flap, and Dan went in. "Thank you," he said automatically, startling the ser-

geant, who probably couldn't have been more surprised if Jackson Houston had suddenly spoken fluent
Swahili. The sergeant followed him in, so that Dan was
wedged between him and the lieutenant. Sourly it occurred to Dan that he was at least in less of a panic than
Jack Houston would have been.

"Well," Flenstein said, "let me tell you the good
news first. It shocks the shit out of me, Private, but after we talked with that girl, it sounds like you actually
rescued her. Might be the first decent thing you ever did
in your life, but you did it. And then on top of that—
well, if you listen to that goofy kid, at least through the
boy that was interpreting for her, it sounds like you held
off the whole German army. Rommel didn't *really* show
up, did he?"

Dan laughed a little. "There were twelve or fifteen of
them, Lieutenant, and they were on an exposed slope.
I had decent cover and a lot of luck."

Flenstein nodded slowly.

"You're a good shot," Scott pointed out. "We've
always given you that."

"That helped, too. But it was pretty close. I was glad
the rest of you turned up."

Huddled there in the now-steamy tent, three men
jammed elbow to elbow, he was warm for the first time
in the day, but he also felt the cold sinking feeling that
comes when two people with absolute power over your
life stare at you as if you've gone insane. He realized,
checking his memories, that Jackson Houston had al-

ways been the positive-attitude kid, the one who tried
to get through by showing how enthusiastic he was
without actually doing anything. If Jackson Houston
had done this, he wouldn't have been attributing it to
luck. He'd have been bucking for a medal.

"Well, then let's finish with the good news," Flenstein said, "because I have some other ground that I
want to cover. You know we kept you here for your
scouting skills and because you're a sniper. You also
know that you've been such a problem for us that we
were talking about sending you home. And home in
your case would eventually mean the stockade, because believe me, buddy, just the things I know about
are enough to send you up to a court-martial and into
the pen for the rest of your life. And I don't think
you're any stranger to jail, whatever you told the draft
board."

Dan's stomach rolled over. He still had no idea what
he was doing or how he had gotten here, and Italy in
February, 1944, was not a vacation spot. But he also
knew, in the same way that he had known things as he
floated in the Wind Between Time, that he belonged
with a fighting unit, not standing trial somewhere a
hundred miles behind the lines.

Flenstein had given that time to sink in, and then he
sighed. "Well, after this afternoon's action I'm not going to send you back. And I was planning to, so don't
kid yourself that this one wasn't close. Now, are you
going to straighten up and fly right?"

"I'll do my best, sir," Dan said. "I appreciate getting one more chance."

From the way Lieutenant Flenstein and Sergeant Scott looked at each other, Dan knew he'd just done something else that wasn't anything like the Private Jack Houston they knew. He pressed into his memory for a moment and had it. They were expecting him to whine about how unfair the whole thing was or to try to bargain it into some "better deal." Well, Jack Houston had just reformed, whether he liked it or not. You might say he was a new man.

Dan just hoped the others would find that out eventually, because the load of hatred his former incarnation had built up was a lot more than Samson wanted to carry.

Scott broke the tension first with a little wry smile. "Are you feeling okay, Houston? You aren't talking much like yourself."

"I don't think anyone could be more surprised than me, Sergeant." It was the truth, anyway.

"Now," Flenstein said, "I would really like to get the truth out of you on one point, Houston. What the hell were you and Bronski doing up there?" He held up a hand as if warding off an expected barrage of rapid-fire lies. "Don't bother to invent anything," he added. "And for God's sake don't cover for your slimy buddy. He might have been the only friend you had here, but a guy who would rape a young girl like that—"

Dan nodded slowly. "We weren't really friends," he said, and let it go at that because that was true, too. "Well, I was out on the usual, recon and maybe some kraut hunting." That actually had been his mission. "I guess I was kind of surprised when Bronski wanted to come along, since usually he isn't, uh, wasn't, the volunteer type."

Jack Houston *had* been surprised. He hadn't realized that Bronski knew about his newly acquired possession or that he would be turning the pressure on for Houston to sell him the first time.

"Anyway, we split up. I don't know if he met the girl in the village or what. We were supposed to meet up at that little shack. I got there, I took a look around—" he shrugged "—and I heard the noises from inside. That kid doesn't look a day older than my baby sister. I got seriously pissed off." Dan paused, realizing he hadn't sounded right for the '40s, but they still seemed to be listening. "I went in to help her out, we had an argument and he ran out the door without looking first. I guess a big part of it was my fault, Lieutenant. We shouldn't have gotten so wrapped up in arguing that we forgot there's a war on." Dan still could not restrain himself when he thought of it. "But, shit, sir, she was just a child. And when I came in he was torturing her, you know? Like scaring her would make it more fun?"

Flenstein nodded soberly. "In my psychology courses they taught me to call that sadomasochism. Out here I guess I'll just say he was a rotten bastard who saved us the bother of a trial. No, I can understand you getting upset, Houston, any man has his limits. And I hope this whole thing will turn over a new leaf for you, because if it doesn't, you're going to be missing the victory parades for the next three wars while you finish out your stockade time."

Inwardly Dan winced. He was one victory parade shy already, as far as he was concerned.

The lieutenant seemed to be satisfied that he had made enough of an impression and said, "Okay, stay here a minute or two. I have some other people to talk to and may need you here for it. Sarge, go get the Count, and I guess after that we'll see this Colonel Turenne."

Sergeant Scott looked at Private Houston with one more withering glare of contempt, a last chance to tell him that the lieutenant was an obvious softy giving him far more of a break than he deserved, and then slipped out the tent door.

"Two more weeks, Houston, and it's rest camp in Naples. Sun. Showers. Sleeping in."

Dan nodded. "Yeah. I've seen all the mud and ice I ever want to." He was trying to sound natural, as if he belonged there, but he was beginning to get tired. It had been a long day no matter how you looked at it. Maybe "home," whatever that was—the warm, friendly place Solly Planyard had apparently gone to?—was ahead of him, but right now he'd have settled for some macaroni and cheese in his tiny efficiency apartment, or better yet, for smuggling a couple of cans of beer into the dollar movies with Sarah. Home was a long way away.

And Jack Houston was really beginning to get to him. He sympathized strongly with Sergeant Scott, and thought that the big Arkansawyer was dead right—this was the best candidate for jail he'd ever encountered. In Vietnam, when he had been a sergeant, it had been easy to rotate a rotten soldier out, and he'd never have had a man like Jack Houston in his unit any longer than it took to get the paperwork done. Out here a man had to go back with the next mule train, which could mean a three-day wait, then four and a half days down the road to the positions around Cassino, which was still a front-line position. It took another day by jeep, after more administrative processing that no one had time for, before he could be started off to Naples and the court-martial he so richly deserved. During the whole trip, of course, a man like Houston would have to be guarded, taking at least one other man off the overstrained front line.

With a cold chill Dan realized that before he had gotten here, the best thing Jackson Houston could have done for the whole Fifth Army was to get killed and not leave enough body to bother shipping down.

The lieutenant seemed to be preoccupied with the map, and that left Dan a little time to think, to sort through Houston's memories and get oriented. Downstream the creek joined the Volturno. The front line— that was a weird idea, he thought, since his Vietnam experience was that the enemy was everywhere. But Houston seemed quite clearly to think of everything except the "front" as safe, except from bombing attacks. Dan's mind was wandering again, and he paused to sort his thoughts out. To the east, over the Apennines, was the British Eighth Army, which was holding positions mostly along the Sangro river, reaching as far up as Ortona along the coast. To the west, "Mark Clark's Fifth Army," as the reporters kept calling it, reached much farther north, to where it was stalled at the Rapido River just below Monte Cassino....

Oh, God. The Rapido. Where the Thirty-sixth had gotten cut to pieces trying to get across. Now he remembered. The platoon had been part of the forces trying to supply covering fire for that hopeless effort to get a bridge for tanks across the swollen river, right under the heavily defended mountain where the Germans had turned the old monastery into a forward observation post for artillery. In three bloody days, just three weeks before, they had lost so much that the unit was pulled back from the line, but since this platoon was still intact, it had been rotated into the supposedly softer duty of guarding the center.

Central Italy was so rugged that even in summer no one could have moved an army north or south through there. The main danger was that small units might make their way through to raid the other sides behind the lines. Officially the Fifth Army's lines ended at Colli al Volturno, but platoon- and squad-sized patrols were constantly out in this country, guarding against German infiltration, and the enemy had similar operations going on their side. Fifty miles east the Eighth Army's patrols were out, as well. In another week they were supposed to rendezvous with one of them north of Agnone, having swept their sector of the Apennines for German troops.

When enemy patrols met, there was a fight. That was what had happened this afternoon. Hopefully the patrol they had run into was a short-range one, and they had seen all there was of it, because if it was part of a long-range patrol comparable in size to their own, they might have to fight a small, nasty, running war for several days on foot across the rocky spine of Italy.

Dan was startled out of his reverie by the entrance of a big, perfectly groomed man. He was wearing a cap, what looked like a drum major's uniform, and riding boots. Dan decided that if this was a hallucination, it had just veered from the grimly real to the utterly bizarre.

The man who stooped into the tent, illuminated by the last colorless light of the day, was tall and slim and would have looked elegant in a tux. Even now, with a little mud splashed around the edges of his finery, he was an imposing figure. His black hair and mustache were perfectly in place. His blue eyes glinted like the steel of a Czech pistol. The cast of his face suggested that he was used to being obeyed and that he enjoyed this fact enormously.

"Count Cabrini," Lieutenant Flenstein said formally. "You'll pardon me if I don't stand."

The lieutenant's head, seated on the ground as he was, was in fact less than an inch from the canvas above, but the irony seemed lost on the count, who was bent more than double but clearly was not going to put his hands down and crawl in on all fours no matter how much sense it might have made.

"I understand there was a difficulty with one of my tenants," the count said. "Or rather with his daughter. He seemed quite upset. I am afraid that one of your men may have attempted to take liberties with a young girl." His English was good, but very formal. There was a touch of Oxford or Cambridge to it, which suggested he must have spent a few years in Britain.

The lieutenant nodded. "I've been investigating that incident myself. The guilty party ran into a dispute with German troops immediately afterward, as you may have heard, and is dead. This is our only witness."

The count turned the full, cold power of his stare on Dan. "And what can you tell me about all of this?"

Dan told the story as straightforwardly as he could, subject always to the count's probing questions. At first he was inclined to like a man who went to so much trouble on his tenant's behalf, but two things began to change his mind. First of all, some of the count's questions seemed to dwell on details that he didn't think had much to do with it. "And this girl, you say, is *very* young under her clothes? And was her pretty face quite distorted with pain, or did it seem to you that this was what you would call an 'act,' that she was waking to pleasure as this corporal touched her?''

"I really don't think that poor kid wanted to be raped," Dan said. "I think she was scared out of her mind."

"Ah, but you and I are men of the world, are we not, sir? And I myself was a soldier in the last war, and we all know that when the thin, lacy trappings of civilization are abruptly torn away... there are some things soldiers know that no civilian, no stay-at-home, ever can learn." Count Cabrini actually winked at him, and the cruelty in his smile chilled Dan's blood.

But since he was getting nowhere with that line of questioning, the count switched tactics, and that was, if anything, worse because every other question from the count would be followed by Flenstein's glance to Samson, telling him clearly that this was not to be answered. What Cabrini was asking, apparently in all innocence, were the kind of question that led to answers that expanded into little additional pieces of information... like where the patrol was headed, what the rendezvous point was, how many signs of Germans had they seen, how many mule trains would be passing through. The last time Dan had been questioned so cleverly, it had been by a B-girl in Saigon.

But she hadn't gotten any information out of him, either, and Cabrini was much less his type. After a while, with no show of frustration, Cabrini turned to

Flenstein and said, "I see that you have prepared your man admirably, and I am wasting my time trying to get any information or to find out what dishonor has been done to my tenant and his family. I suppose one might expect your people to stick together." He got up and left without another word.

"Fuck," the lieutenant said firmly. He socked one hand into another.

Dan couldn't think of a polite way to ask, so he just sighed and said, "Nice guys they have up here, sir. You want to bet he rapes her himself before the month is out?"

Flenstein nodded. "No takers. That's a sucker bet." He sat quietly for a moment and then said, "And just so you won't be mystified, Private, when he said 'your people,' he has the impression that any American from a big city is a Jew."

Sergeant Scott came back in, overhearing the last of it, and said, "That's okay, Lieutenant. I think after he heard my accent he was trying to get me to put on my sheet and come up the hill for a cross-burning."

Flenstein laughed. "Is our French colonel here yet? Nothing personal, but I'd like to get Houston here out of my tent before we end up either with our flesh grown together or married under Italian law."

"Just coming up the hill now, sir." There was something odd about Scott's voice, something Houston had little memory of, and Dan, of course, had none. "I think he ran here with a full kit."

Admiration—that was it.

Turenne himself was a short, compact man who looked as if he had borrowed de Gaulle's nose and mustache to mount on his own wide, flat face. He was built like a good wrestler or judo man, and he moved with the kind of quiet assurance that clearly said he had taken the measure of the world around him, and big as it might be, he was big enough for it.

He arrived with two full thermoses of hot coffee, and after refusing any for himself, bestowed them as gifts on Flenstein and Scott.

Dan decided that this was someone he wanted to know, but then Turenne glanced at him and gave him a sneer of contempt that changed Dan's mind right away. He probed around in Jackson Houston's memory and realized there were probably a thousand good reasons for Turenne to despise him.

Hadn't Jackson Houston made one real friend, won the loyalty of one real comrade? How was Dan supposed to accomplish whatever it was that he had been sent back to this time for, when his past incarnation had already made such a thorough mess of everything? Or why couldn't he have come back five years before, say, right after Houston was released from that one-year stretch in the Illinois State Reform School, and had enough time to make something of this guy?

He realized how tired he was. After all, from one viewpoint there had been more than forty years in this day already.

Turenne and Flenstein exchanged a few more pleasantries, squatting there in the tent. Then Flenstein turned to Samson and said, "I think you have some things you need to talk about with the colonel. I suggest the two of you go somewhere private to talk about them." Gripping Samson's arm, he added, "If you behave like you've been behaving these last few hours, you might come through it all right, and you'll like yourself better anyway. And you had better understand this—no one will lift a finger to help you. Now go with the colonel."

Turenne turned his back and headed over the ridge line. Dan followed him, knowing he would not enjoy what was coming. As they came up the ragged edge, Turenne went over low and cautiously. Dan followed suit, the rough stones and gravel scraping against his boots. A cold wind had sprung up with the dying day, and even the brief breaking of sunlight on the slope failed to bring any warmth.

Turenne turned to face him, and, with no trace of expression, hit him with the full force of that compact, muscular body, a hard blow directly into Dan's face.

5

Knowing the number of things he was guilty of—or that Jackson Houston was guilty of—Dan figured Turenne was entitled to this, and he left his arms at his sides as he was hit again and again until he fell to his knees. Turenne kicked him from behind. The gravel, broken by a patch of dead brown grass, flew up and scraped Dan's bruised face. The Frenchman's boots thudded into Samson's ribs, a hollow booming of pain, yet held in check just enough not to crack a rib and put Dan out of action. This was a punishment, not a fight, and much as it hurt, Dan understood that it was intended to leave him in condition to fight.

The kicks and blows rained down, missing the vital areas, never hard enough to do serious or permanent injury, but guaranteeing that Dan would be sore in the days to come. Again and again he thought he was at last numb and beyond pain, and again and again Turenne found some new way to hurt, something to make him ache again. But he did not cry out, he did not scream and he did not resist. It was not pride nor protest, but just that Dan could not see that it would gain either him or Colonel Turenne anything. When at last Turenne was panting from the effort of having battered him and Dan was aching everywhere he possibly could, the colonel said quietly, "I suppose you will want to know why I have done this."

"I can think of several reasons," Dan said, gasping at the soreness of his ribs, "and you're within your rights."

"Yes, I am," Turenne said. "And I will tell you how much I am within my rights. You are the one who ran your clever black market back at Colli, no? You are the one that was supplying girls to my men—and a few miles away the same girls were working for the Germans. Do you follow me so far?"

"Yes," Dan said. He was still on the ground. His face was directly by Turenne's boot, and he wondered if the next beating would begin with the crash of that road-dusty boot into his teeth. He tried not to flinch from it, for he knew that if anything could infuriate Turenne more, it would be any show of cowardice.

"One of those girls learned a name. And the name went to a German. And from that German to more Germans, until it reached a German in Cherbourg. Where, it so happened, the lieutenant whose name it was had a wife. You will note I say had."

"Oh, God." Dan had meant to stay passive, but now he could not bear it. His stomach rolled over, and he vomited there on the ground in front of himself, the brown puddle forming on the gravel.

He felt the hard, icy press of Turenne's boot on the back of his neck. He could not have resisted it, and perhaps he didn't want to. My God, my God, he cried mentally, what have I been in this life? What must I do to pay this back?

As if Turenne had heard him, without removing his boot and keeping Samson's face planted firmly in the vomit-wet ground, he said, "You can give me something that might atone, a little. There is something you can do for me."

"Name it, sir, please," Dan whispered. He was afraid he might throw up again, but he didn't seem to have anything else to do it with. The icy ground was almost soothing. The stench in his nostrils made him want to faint, to slip into blackness and never wake up.

"You know of the German retaliations against the Maquis, the Resistance fighters? They oftentimes shoot ten innocent people in retaliation for one Boche death. You know of this?" He took his boot off Samson's head.

Dan nodded, pushing himself up onto his hands a little and drawing a sweet lungful of clean air.

"That is my price, Houston, you pig. Give me ten dead Boche by dawn, and I may begin to think of you as human."

It was plain that Turenne expected him to crawl away, whimpering. That, as much as the debt he felt, made Daniel Samson say, "Okay. Ten or more. By dawn."

Turenne squatted and looked at him with curiosity. "Do you mean this?"

"Ten," Dan repeated. Hell, the terrain was different, as was the climate, but it would be a lot like the

one-man missions they'd sent him off to accomplish in
Nam—and he'd feel cleaner after doing it. He stood up,
pulled the greasy rag from his pocket and wiped his face
with it, but his mind was frantically searching through
Jackson Houston's memories, looking for something
that would give him a way...

Aha. This was Houston's third long-range patrol out
here, and being the sort that he was, he'd done some
trading across the lines, the usual sort of petty Ameri-
can-cigarettes-for-German-canned-ham stuff just to
keep his hand in. Far away from his unit's prying eyes,
he had actually been back into enemy territory a little...and now he remembered something.

"I think," he said, "that with a three-hour walk,
mostly north, we might be able to surprise a German
radar. Looked like a mobile rig, not too different from
ours, probably a couple of platoons guarding and op-
erating it, if it's still there—but it probably is, keeping
an eye on flights across the peninsula."

"You have some plan for this?"

"Yeah, in this weather the guards are probably none
too alert, and it's far enough back I'd bet they even have
a fire going. Easy to find. When we do, we get through
the sentries—that ought to get me one German right
there—and then, if we can find the technicians' quarters, we get them next, since they're the ones the Germans would find hardest to replace. With a little luck
they'll be bunked with the officers. A guy in the unit,
uh, owes me a favor, so I think I can probably take

along a BAR and some extra grenades. Three hours or a bit less to get there, twenty minutes to hit, and we can rejoin the patrol at the next stop—there's a flat patch eight miles up the hill that I bet is Flenstein's next campsite.''

''You say 'we.' ''

''Would you take *my* word about how many Germans I had killed?''

''An excellent point.'' The solid little Frenchman thought for a long moment. ''I do not think it likely I have misjudged you. But I think it would be good if we tried to do this, in any case. The loss of a radar will help blind their air operations for a few days, and I know that my unit would appreciate a bit less dive-bombing and strafing. I had planned to make this patrol with your Lieutenant Flenstein anyway, because we will be taking over the responsibility from you when your unit is rotated elsewhere, and I need to know the territory. But I can learn it quite well traveling with you, I suppose.

''All right, then, the offer is accepted if we can leave tonight.''

Samson was already tired, but he also understood instinctively that if he didn't carry this one off, or even if he complained, he would be screwing up whatever as yet unknown thing he was supposed to accomplish. ''You got it. Let me get another K ration swallowed—I seem to have lost one.''

Turenne snorted. Perhaps he wasn't totally devoid of a sense of humor after all. They walked back to camp together, and while Turenne went to square things with Flenstein, Dan got himself fed again and called in the necessary favors. In less than an hour they were ready to go.

"I don't think your lieutenant much liked knowing that his next campsite was so predictable," Turenne commented. "But I think finding out that it is, is fundamentally healthy for him and everyone else."

Dan nodded. He looked down the slope, beyond the little farmhouse where he had first found himself in 1944, and where Bronski had died, and into the dark valley beyond. The moon would be up in another hour, a help to them if they were far enough along by then, a help to the German patrol if they were still too close.

Dan carried the BAR and all the ammunition he thought he safely could. He had checked, and Houston's memories of how to work one seemed solid enough. In addition, he had four small charges and half a dozen grenades. It wasn't the lightest load, but it would make him fairly formidable, and at least with Turenne's tommy gun, scrounged from someplace or other, they would be able to lay down a decent rate of fire. He was still trying to imagine that the men around him had been in combat all the way from North Africa—actually most of them had been there for the first landings in Morocco—with only a semiauto weapon. If, somehow, he ever ended up back in his own time, maybe he'd be a little nicer to the guys at the Veterans of Foreign Wars meetings.

Then again, the Germans were mostly firing single rounds, too.

As they moved down the slope, cautiously and quietly, he searched through Houston's memories to make sure he had the right route.

It was dark and frightening the whole way. Nearly empty countryside with no more than starlight is darker than almost anywhere else. Too, the cold was now fierce, searing Samson's lungs and making his toes sting as he battered them against the stony hillsides. The crisp coldness seemed to magnify every sound, so that he thought sometimes they must be able to hear him in Berlin, and he was painfully aware that, careful as they were to stay off skylines, he was visible for a good long way. In Vietnam the complaint had been that you couldn't see. Here it was that you could always be seen.

The poor bastards who had tried to cross the Rapido had been visible from the break of dawn until, days later, they had been pulled back. And in Italy to be seen was to be shot at.

Behind him, Turenne was grim and silent as a ghost. *Maybe, after we get this done, he'll just kill me out here. By his lights, I'd have it coming,* Samson thought. *No, he's the Boy Scout type. In more ways than one—I've never seen a guy so quiet in country.*

Once, crossing a lonely track, too undeveloped to be designated even as a jeep trail, they were forced to dive

for a ditch as a German motorcycle messenger roared
by. The moment he was gone, Dan rose, uncoiled some
of the bell wire that he always carried, and strung it between a tree and a signpost, about neck high.

"Good trick," Turenne whispered. "A pity we won't
be here to see him surprised. Did you go to OSS school,
or have you worked with the Maquis?"

Perhaps because they were the first friendly, or at
least neutral, words from Turenne, Dan accidentally
blurted out the truth. "A friend in Earth First."

Turenne smiled very slightly, his front teeth glinting
in the moonlight. "You're right, of course. We need to
get a few Boche under the ground before conversing."

The last two miles were a slow uphill climb along the
side of a steep ridge that came off the mountain where
Dan had seen the radar. They circled around for another twenty minutes, getting the radar up against the
moon, and then slowly crawled forward.

This wasn't much different from Special Forces
school—in fact it was more like his training, in the early
'60s, than what Dan had actually encountered in Vietnam. The guard below him was standing on one of the
few flat patches, and though he was probably supposed to be patrolling, his legs by now had gotten tired
and sore, so he stayed on his rock and stared off into the
landscape. Every so often he shivered and stamped,
giving his position away. When he did that, Dan almost felt a little sympathy, until he realized this guy was
even bigger than he was.

When he sprang on the guard, it was strictly by the book. There was the anxious instant as the loop of fine wire flipped forward over the low, squat helmet, the hairbreadth of heart-stopping time when he yanked the handles and felt no tension, saw the German's hands begin to rise reflexively, and then the firm resistance on the handles as he tightened down, turning sideways so that he could draw on the handles like a longbow, squeezing the throat in the first instant so that there was no sound and in the next crushing the larynx and beginning the panic as pain lanced through the guard's head, so that the guard's rifle would have fallen with a clatter if Dan had not already forced him down . . .

Then he wrapped his legs around the guard, bracing his boots on the struggling, silently screaming man's pelvis, sitting back as if dragging the German soldier onto his lap, and sharply arching his back, pushing his hips against the German's back and hauling back on the wire. The wire bit deep, sliced flesh . . . blood flowed from the thin line left by the garrote as it sliced clear through to the spine under the force of Samson's thrust, shoving the German's body down with his feet and hauling his head up by the wire.

It wasn't as neat as what you saw in old Commando flicks, where you just squeezed their necks and they fell dead—but this worked.

The German was unconscious; he would be dead and freezing in a minute or two, and nothing could save or revive him now—only bolt cutters could take that wire off his neck. As Dan let go and climbed out from under the body, the head lolled to the side and the great swell from the severed jugular and carotid poured forth.

One, Dan thought. He moved forward along the line of the hill, angling upward again until he was above the next guard.

This one was on gravel, not the stone the other one had chosen, and the risk of noise was greater. Dan's hand whipped over the man's mouth and nose, pinching the nostrils to trigger a breath panic and bring the man's hands up, then stabbed twice, hard, sliding the blade into the guard's back, up under the floating ribs, sideways through the kidneys, maybe nicking the liver or intestine or spinal cord as well, two hard thrusts that doomed him while he still fought to pry Dan's hand free from his face.

As the hands dropped, Dan's knife whipped around front, between the man's legs, finding the top of the thigh muscle and slicing deep, biting into the flesh and down to the bone, severing the femoral artery... turning and cutting through to the same artery on the other leg, castrating him on the way.

The guard was past caring, unconscious from the sudden loss of blood pressure in the brain, and his hands had already fallen twitching to his sides. For insurance, Samson made the fifth cut and thumped the knife in below the sternum, through coat, skin, diaphragm, lung, and heart and felt the body go completely limp. The time taken for the five deadly thrusts and cuts was less than three seconds, still well within standards.

That made two. Having a twenty-year-old body helped, he realized, but he was amazed at how well he'd stayed in training.

Since he'd heard no sound, Dan assumed that Turenne must be almost done, as well.

"Fine knife work," the Frenchman breathed in his ear. Dan was momentarily proud that he hadn't jumped. Turenne had come up so quietly that he hadn't perceived him. "And I saw the other. My two are also off to hell to await their friends. Let us not keep them waiting...you owe me eight."

"Right."

The antenna itself was being aimed by two bored Germans who had a tiny tin-can gasoline stove, the type that Houston had seen a thousand of, and sat hunched and warming their hands over it. If he'd had an infrared sight, he could have taken them out at a thousand yards, but he wasn't sure those were invented yet. Hell, for that matter, while he was at it he could wish for a Stinger or a TOW to take the whole thing out from two mountains away.

The antenna was a dish of heavy metal wire that looked like a chicken-wire sculpture Sarah had done during her artistic period, or maybe like the armature for the ears on a giant plaster Mickey Mouse. Cables led to a phone by the men. One large cable led from the antenna down into the ground.

"This makes it complicated," he breathed in Turenne's ear. "Everything important is underground. We'll have to go in after them."

"What do you know about radar? It's supposed to be classified—"

"Previous assignment," Dan breathed. Damn! He'd forgotten that in 1944 people knew what radar was, but how it worked was classified. "There's at least a couple of truckloads of other crap, and several technicians, that ought to be here, too. Almost for sure they're down under in a cave. That antenna's the only thing that has to be up here—those two goons are just to aim it."

Turenne nodded. "I'm glad you're here. I say we need a free hand first. Let's rush the two fools over their fire."

This time they did it together, with bayonets, a hard thrust at the base of the skull that Dan had learned half a lifetime ago, and that his instructor had probably learned someplace like this. They were less careful of noise, for there was no one to hear them out here, though they had to avoid gunfire.

Moments later they were wiping their bayonets on the Germans' greatcoats.

The Jackson Houston part of his mind suggested seeing what kind of loot there might be. Dan had no trouble resisting the thought.

On close inspection, the cable led to a pipe that seemed to go into the hill at an angle. Farther down the hill, among rocks, they saw something gleam and move and disappear, then gleam again.

Dan realized what it must be. It was good that they had been quiet before. He crept slowly down the hill, Turenne at his side. The German guard at the cave mouth was smoking. It was a truly stupid thing to do at night, but out here there could easily have been no one around for fifty miles, and not everyone on either side took sentry duty very seriously.

Seeing his dangling chin straps as they peered two feet from the back of his head, Dan gestured to Turenne, who nodded, leaned forward, and at Dan's signal, plucked the helmet off the guard's head.

The guard had just a moment of frozen shock at being touched when he had thought he was alone, then began to stammer what Dan figured was the German for "Sorry, chief, it won't happen again," as the butt of Dan's BAR fractured his skull.

"This is not a drill," Dan murmured.

It was icy cold now and past midnight as they slipped into the cave in the mountain, leaving behind even the dim, occasional light of the moon. After twenty feet it was warmer, and in a little while, as they crept forward, holding hands like kids in a movie so they wouldn't lose each other, it was perceptibly warm and even a little stuffy. Apparently there were quite a few people down there, and the ventilation system could not quite cope with it.

Another turn brought dim light to their eyes, filtering around a big piece of blackout curtain. Two more turns and two more curtains, and they could hear voices. A quieter side corridor opened, and they went down that way.

"You were right," Turenne breathed. "This is a really large facility."

"Too big," Dan whispered back. "Radar should take up one big room. There's more here than just that."

He checked his watch. They had forty minutes to do whatever they were going to do if they wanted an hour's darkness to get away in. And he still owed Turenne seven, maybe eight, dead Germans.

As long as he was bagging Germans, he'd rather get some Nazis and some officers. These were pretty clearly garrison troops and not very good ones, though what they were doing in the Apennines, in that case, became a really interesting question.

"Hear that hum?" he whispered. "Generator. If we take that out and do it right, we ought to shut this place down for a while. Let's see if we can get there."

A single German guard dozed by the thrumming diesel engine. He died there, perhaps thinking it was only a bad dream, but in any case without raising any cry.

Turenne moved to shut the engine off, but Dan stopped him. He had seen the drive belt disappearing into the wall from the other side of the diesel, and, sure enough, looking through the slit for the belt he saw that on the other side there was a fan. This was all the ventilation the cave had.

"Beautiful," he whispered. The exhaust and air intake for the diesel were two parallel pipes running up the side of the ventilation shaft—the diesel drew air from outside through one tube, returned its exhaust through the other, and everything that breathed below drew air from around those two pipes. Break the pipes, and it would all mix. He placed his first charge there, and lit the fuse—thirty seconds.

He spun around, grabbed the toolbox from the bench, opened it and pitched the loose mix of screwdrivers and wrenches into the generator's open end. There were screams, groans and bangs as the generator armature shed pieces of coil, and then the lights went out. In the dark he could hear only the howl of the generator, now lopsided, shaking itself to pieces, and he and Turenne got out of the room an instant before the charge ruptured the intake and exhaust lines. The diesel engine, spinning out of control without the load of the generator, was now drawing air and expelling exhaust into the cave system, its fan whirring madly as it did so. It would shortly be unbreathable as diesel exhaust filled the cave.

"That will stir them up," he shouted in Turenne's ear. Faint red lights flickered on as battery power brought them up. "Now let's go out through the main part. Make sure you shoot anyone who isn't wearing a uniform. It's most likely a civilian technician, and those are scarcer and harder to replace.''

Turenne nodded, and the two of them pounded down the hallway, trying now to find rather than avoid the largest rooms.

They emerged in a gallery overlooking what was obviously, even in the pallid flickering, a charting room, where a huge map of central Italy covered the great table in the center of the room. About twenty people with what looked like shuffleboard sticks stood anxiously around it, waiting while a man in a suit spoke on the phone, obviously demanding to know the cause of the power failure.

Dan pitched two grenades over the railing, braced his BAR into a corner of the railing to hold it down and sprayed the crowd with bullets. He saw several fall. Firing two short bursts, Turenne cut down the man at the phone and another who was running for the door.

No one had returned fire yet. Perhaps no one in the facility was armed.

Back in the corridor the stench of diesel exhaust was overpowering. They held their breath and kicked the next door open on the other side of the corridor.

It was the radar room. A few men milled around in confusion while others shouted orders. The screens, now blind and dark, sat untended. Dan unslung the BAR and sprayed the room once. He popped the clip and sprayed again. It was a lot of ammunition to use, and his shoulder ached from wrestling thirty pounds of bucking weapon. Half the rounds must have gone into the ceiling, but he figured pretty nearly everyone in the room was hit, probably several dead, and better still, he'd probably shattered a lot of expensive vacuum tubes. To make sure that continued, he rushed into the room, opened the little doors on the back of the big metal electronics cabinets, chucked two grenades in and dived away.

Turenne's tommy gun roared deafeningly in the small room, cutting down an officer who had been standing up with a pistol as Dan rolled out. Turenne tackled him, and they hit the floor as the radar room equipment went up with a roar.

"But that's supposed to be a three-second fuse," Dan said.

Turenne laughed. Obviously he thought that was a joke.

So did Jackson Houston's memory. Out here three seconds meant anywhere from one-half to seven seconds. Rumor had it all the new-model, reliable grenades were going to the Pacific.

Dan would have laughed himself, but the fires they had started were making it hard to breathe, and there was no telling how long the battery power would keep the place lighted. He could hear the engine shrieking like a cat on fire now, and when it flamed and died, it would probably set a fire at the end of its fuel lines and blaze up enough to kill anyone left in the cave from smoke inhalation.

"Time to get out, but let's not waste any grenades," Turenne shouted in his ear, echoing his thoughts.

Death walked through the secret Nazi base in the cave that night.

As they made their way to the surface, they found ventilator shafts, open doors or doors they could open with a burst of automatic fire, and in went the grenades. The cave was full of screams and wails. The wounded, the dying, the suffocating, those on fire and the merely terrified.

Samson pivoted at one turn, his last charge ready, kicked the door open, pitched it in and slammed the door.

A picture registered in his mind of a sleepy, older man, probably some poor leftover from the First World War, nodding over his newspaper on the toilet, jerking awake as the door was kicked in and staring in astonishment as a grenade dropped between his feet.

Daniel Samson had just time to turn back, as if he could do anything, when the door flew outward...

He made himself not look and kept going.

The corridor leading out of the mountain was jammed with people, many of them not in uniform. Dan dived to prone—the only position in which the BAR could really be controlled—and slowly worked the crowd, mowing them down like so much wheat in a hailstorm. Beside him, Turenne chewed into them, the big .45-caliber slugs bursting people apart, most of them falling forward in waves as others ran into the freezing night in shirtsleeves and lab coats. As one man, the two rose and rushed forward. A couple of stray pistol shots rang out, and Samson slapped in another clip and sprayed again.

They were out into the night. Dan fed one of his last three clips in and fired a burst into the back of a fleeing German. With a small charge, Turenne ran to where the smoke poured from the once-concealed opening of the ventilator shaft. A moment later, with a boom of high explosives, that was sealed. Those left inside would suffocate within minutes if they did not get to the doorway.

Dan leveled the BAR in prone firing position on the entrance to the cave and waited. Something moved twice, and he fired. Once it might have been smoke, but the other time there was a cry of human agony.

Turenne squatted beside him. "Total victory. And in less than an hour."

Dan sighed. "Yeah. Unarmed troops and half of them civilians. But—" he pointed at the radar dish "—they might just have been the most dangerous people out here."

The Frenchman shook his head. "An installation like this . . . to watch for aircraft when they cannot do anything about them? To track movements of mere dots on a screen? No, this must have some other purpose, my friend. There is something out there, perhaps back at Kesselring's HQ, perhaps quite near, that this was in support of. Something so important that they would build such a facility just to support it. You see what I mean? They are up to something in central Italy . . . and we will know what it is, to our sorrow, quite possibly too late." He gave Dan a hard clap on the shoulder. "I don't know if you have my interest in physical culture, but if you are willing, I would like to *run* back to our rendezvous point. There is something mysterious going on out here, and Lieutenant Flenstein and his men should be apprised of that . . . as, indeed, perhaps everyone should."

"I could get into that, sir," Dan said, grimly glad that he'd expended so much ordnance in this massacre and therefore would not need to lug it back. All the same, a BAR was still thirty pounds.

"Interesting expression—American?"

"Excuse me, sir?"

"You said 'I could get into that.' That's not a common expression in English, at least not to me, and I think I'm a bit of a scholar and speak English rather well—don't disillusion me on that point, my friend. So I thought, perhaps, an Americanism . . ."

"It might be." Dan took a deep breath. He couldn't remember anyone saying "I could get into that" when he had been a child, so perhaps it was American. In any case, it was certainly a new expression. "I guess we'd better start this run. And on this ground we really need to take it easy."

They began at an almost-gentle dogtrot, under the sinking moon, the icy claws of the February air tearing at Dan's lungs, his breath billowing out in great clouds. He was tired. He had been up almost twenty-four hours. He was exhausted—he had been in battle twice. He was hurt from the beating Turenne had given him earlier.

But he was glowing with pleasure from two words of Turenne's.

My friend.

What beautiful words.

6

They actually beat Flenstein and the platoon to the
rendezvous. It was less of a surprise when Dan realized
how much more gear even a stripped platoon had to
carry, and moreover that the mules tended to be geared
to the long, slow crossings they had been doing since
Caesar had come this way as a young man, rather than
the hurry-up approach occasioned by the presence of
modern, mechanized warfare and modern, mechanized Americans.

As they sat at the meeting point, sometimes dozing in
the rising sun of an unusually warm, clear day, Turenne talked. Dan knew after a while that Turenne simply liked to talk and that an enlisted man of an allied
army was good enough if nobody else was handy, but
he didn't mind much. The Frenchman was interesting,
a cultivated gentleman of the old school, graduate of St.
Cyr who could discuss any subject, from how Clause-
witz would have interpreted force dispositions at Wa-
terloo, Chickamauga or Marston Moor, to exactly what
he did and didn't like about the new generation of
French writers, now flourishing partly among the Resistance.

It was good to be alive, good to be fresh from battle
without a scratch or a lost friend, good to know he had

done something to frustrate the Nazis. Someplace he had heard World War II called "The Last Good War," and he understood a bit of what they meant by that right now.

Then Turenne turned thoughtful and quiet, and finally said, "I will have to say something to my fellow officers about all this. That I went up to chastise an American soldier for his stupid, criminal dealings with the black market, that had cost one of my officers his happiness forever. And that I beat him within an inch of his life—so much they will understand. It's later, going out together, this blow we've struck . . . those will be hard to explain."

Daniel Samson had nothing to say at that moment. He felt horrible inside to realize that this, his new, his only, friend, was going to be put to such trouble on his behalf—more so because he knew that it was usually not the job of a colonel to defend a private.

"Well," Turenne said, "there is something I can finish out the story with that may ease them on this matter. It has not been unusual in French history for our heroes to come from—if I may be blunt—the ranks of criminals."

Dan looked sidelong at Turenne, seated beside him on the broad, flat rock, and said nothing. The warm, pale sunlight continued to flood the valley. Patches of snow spread tentacles of rivulets down the valley slope, and the sound of trickling water was everywhere.

"You probably don't know what I am talking about. But the Foreign Legion that we brag about to the world is made up mainly of the world's criminals. This is, of course, not by our choice...any foreigner may enlist...but you know, at the tiny wage, and the isolation, and the policy of the French government of losing legionnaires first, before Frenchmen... Well, no man with common sense enlists in the Legion unless he has nothing to lose and needs a new identity very badly. And because so often they are among the first troops into action, and because they are always sent where danger is very great, they become heroes. Now, you imagine a boy who grows up in the slums..."

Dan reached back and found Jackson Houston living out in Jefferson Parish, near New Orleans, in Gretna, a little sleepy town, in which the Houstons had been, since time immemorial, the trashiest of white trash. During Prohibition his father had displayed enough ambition to move north to Chicago, to a tenement on the South Side, and open up one of the traditional family businesses, dealing with every criminal gang in an absolutely evenhanded way—he sold bad liquor to all of them.

After Prohibition they had eked out a living on the usual family mixture of begging, stealing and sponging. Only Jackson had gotten a high school diploma, and it was widely held among his family that the experience of education had permanently warped him, for he had amazed the family by not trying to dodge the draft. Amazed them again by completing basic, and then flabbergasted them utterly with a combat record that was, in fact, not too shabby. Flenstein, Scott, every officer or sergeant who had dealings with him, had disliked him as a troublemaker and opportunist—the same reasons Daniel Samson didn't like him—but no one questioned his courage or his fighting ability.

He returned from his reverie to see the tiny dots moving quickly over a ridge line on the horizon—men and mules.

"Here they come. God, I hope I still have my shelter half—I'm really looking forward to a little sleep."

Turenne smiled. "Your wish has been granted, I am sure, for I would wager you will get *very* little sleep."

TURENNE WAS absolutely right. Dan didn't know how much sleep he had had, but knowing Turenne and Flenstein, he suspected it was as much as they could spare him. When he was shaken awake, not gently, by Sergeant Scott, the first overwhelming shock that hit was that he was still there. He had expected this to turn out to be a very vivid dream, perhaps in his hospital bed, though he wasn't sure when it had started being a dream—with Master Xi? With Solly Planyard? With that idiot fascist kid slaughtering anyone who threatened to be smarter than he was? Surely, even though all of that was at least remotely possible, finding himself taking over for a previous incarnation in World War II would have to be within the dream.

But how many times in a dream do you fall asleep and then wake up, still tired? And know that you will never wake up back in the life you left?

All this confusion was nothing compared to the shock of what the sergeant told him. "They say they're sorry but they really need you—they had a guy come out from HQ to talk to you. I think he's a spy, so you watch yourself, hear?"

Dan nodded and headed for the lieutenant's tiny pup tent, trying to figure out how HQ could have known anything was up, let alone dispatched anyone. Had Turenne really meant it when he had said that the base with the hidden radar was that significant? Would they have broken radio silence over that?

The long-range patrols across the center of Italy were usually isolated for the full week until they met up with the Eighth Army patrols, Mark Clark's men from the western side of Italy linking up, briefly, with Leese's from the east. Virtually all of the time, in that vast empty land, the Allied and Nazi patrols missed each other completely, and spent their time in wretched holes or tents, developing chronic cases of trench foot or simply trying to stay alive in the bitter cold.

When opposing patrols did meet, men died without any more reason than their own bad luck and the generals' need for reassurance, for the generals were reasonably sure nothing of any military value could be done in central Italy, where supporting even a platoon

overland required great effort, but they were only reasonably sure.

To be surer, they sent out the patrols. When enemy
troops meet, they fight. And when they fight lightly
armed in small units, it becomes a matter of personal,
individual murder of a stranger... which is pointless
from everyone's viewpoint, most of all the stranger's.

Like almost everything in Italy, this was a sideshow
from the "real" war elsewhere, and therefore it seemed
unlikely that anything significant enough to break the
orders for radio silence could be happening.

But then, how likely was it that a Vietnam vet from
the future would be here?

Such thoughts were circling in Daniel Samson's head
as he crossed the ground to the lieutenant's tent. He
noticed that everyone watched him.

The sun was still out, and it was now really warm.
The icy chill still lay on the land, and there were patches
of gray-white slush scabbing over even the sunny parts
of the slopes, but all the same it was a little, mild breath
of spring.

It didn't bother him to be watched. He had been used
to getting stares of hatred. At least these were more
looks of curiosity, with little overt hostility. In a small
military unit people get to have roles, and others come
to depend on them. The clown will have a wisecrack and
will cut up, the iron man will volunteer to bear amaz-
ing loads and will not complain about them, the baseball nut will do anything it takes to get box scores and

will illustrate his conversation with grand slams and bases on balls, and the unit's rat will sneak, lie and cheat.

The baseball nut does not become the iron man, the make-out artist does not become the bookworm.

And the unit rat does not behave unselfishly, does not put himself out for the common good.

They were trying to figure out if there was some dishonest advantage that they couldn't see in what he had done, or if perhaps somehow the world was ending and Jack Houston was not quite what they had thought him to be.

It was a start. Despite his aching muscles and the sore places where Turenne had pounded on him, he felt a lot better at once, knowing that there was now at least hope.

He walked a little taller, but he didn't kid himself. He really needed the good will and friendship of the men of his unit, and Jackson Houston had simply cheated them, lied to them, taken blatant advantage too many times to have much hope for that yet.

The oddest thing was that, in rummaging through so many of his ugly memories, he was beginning to like Houston just a little, to see a tiny touch of promise. The family background, in fact, had been so awful that he was surprised Houston had ever made even a half-decent private. The Houston family's criminal approach to the world might be deeply ingrained, but for some reason Jackson Houston had resisted a little bit.

It wasn't much reason to be proud of a past incarnation, but it was about all there was.

God, he was tired, and his thoughts wandered. He had found out last night that when he was tired, he sometimes said things that made no sense in the present context. He didn't think there was much of a chance anyone here would actually figure out that he was really someone different, from the future, sent back by some unknown power, but it seemed entirely likely that they might add it all together, decide he had some strange belief system he wasn't divulging and invalid him out on a section eight. That, he knew in his strange new way of knowing, would be a disaster.

At Lieutenant Flenstein's pup tent, everybody was sitting on a big, dry rock, and sure enough there was a new man there. He was wearing an Army uniform, but without any insignia. Houston's memory filled in that this was common among the OSS men, many of whom were technically civilians.

"Private Houston, this is Mr. Robert Senneman. He was air-dropped in here after our radio message back to base. He's here to talk to you about what you saw in that mountain. Unfortunately Colonel Turenne doesn't have quite your technical familiarity. In fact, we hadn't known you knew anything about radar."

Dan cleared his throat and thought frantically, trying to come up with something technically true. So far, he had not lied about anything directly, nor really tried to hide any information. "Ah, back when I was right out of basic, before I got into this outfit, um, they had me sweeping a place out. And people there were pretty loose-lipped, you know? So I picked some stuff up, enough to help wreck the place, but not enough to really know what I was seeing. I just figured anything with vacuum tubes was bad.''

Senneman sighed. ''Well, as lucky as we've been, I don't suppose we could have hoped to be lucky enough to have you know more than that. But it's a very good start. Whatever they were up to, they're out of business temporarily, and we now know there's something to look for.'' He pulled out his pipe and tamped down some tobacco. It seemed to take him a while to get it lit, but they all sat quietly while he worked on it. ''Hmm. Well, let me just talk you through the whole action, if you don't mind. And now that you're involved in an Intelligence matter, let me add that you should feel free to venture some ideas and suggestions as you have them—there's no point insisting on rank when what we need are ideas.''

Samson thought they'd all be bored, and tried to shorten things, but Senneman would have none of that. He kept probing. Had there been any unit insignia on the Germans? Had he seen any living quarters for the fifty or sixty people in the base? Was there, or could there have been, a road anywhere? Were there any mast or dish antennae, besides the one for the radar?

It took more than an hour before Senneman sighed and said, ''Well, that takes care of that. It sounds as though it's almost got to be one of their field units, which we've only seen in air photos. We think those are being saved for whenever the second front opens. In a way it's a shame we didn't capture it intact, except I'll be damned if I can see either how we could have gotten it down to base, or for that matter how they could have gotten it up here without being spotted by air reconnaissance.

"Wouldn't that antenna have shown from the air?" Dan asked.

Senneman shook his head. "Probably not. I bet that thing was going inside every night just before dawn. And this whole area is covered by one lonely old Typhoon with two cameras and a noisy engine."

"Skyfart Fred," Lieutenant Flenstein said. "Yeah, everyone in the platoon can tell you just what he sounds like. Not exactly a gadget for sneaking up with. We thought maybe it was a decoy to draw German fighters out over the lines."

"No, I'm afraid it's just a demonstration of what the budget's like up here. On any other front, that contraption would have been retired long ago, but here in Italy you guys get the last and least of everything. So they'd have had no trouble keeping that radar station hidden once it was set up—but to haul all that stuff up here—well, you know better than I do how hard it is to move at all at night. The ground's way too rough and way too slippery. Now try hauling, say, ten or twenty tons of delicate electronics at night without leaving too many tracks—"

"Then what did they do?" Turenne asked. "Surely they didn't bring it in a balloon or build it on the site."

"No need for either. No, what it means is that there are three or four old fascists, or new collaborators in the area, probably aristocrats because that tends to be the way they go, and because they'd be the ones with big enough farms and outbuildings to keep things hidden, and the roads, such as they are, tend to run between their houses.

"The really interesting question is why they'd go to that much trouble and expense. Not just hauling the stuff up, but having to conceal rations coming up for that many people, and for that matter increasing the amount of suspicious activities around the houses of their supporters, maybe risking arrests or partisan raids. All that trouble to put a radar station where all there is to watch is the occasional courier Spitfire plus Skyfart Fred. They might be watching for bombing raids against their Gustav Line positions, but frankly I can't see what the gain in that would be. To send a sneak attack this way, we'd have to plan on sneaking past about ten other installations, and on top of that they'd have to fly practically right down through the passes in this rotten weather."

Senneman looked around at the circle of faces before he continued. "No. That, and all the other electronics they had in there, says just one thing—it's for guidance and navigation. They find the plane and give it its position. You only really need that if you're going to do a pinpoint raid somewhere deep in enemy territory. And more to the point, you wouldn't build a station like that unless you were going to send a *lot* of bombers, and soon, because they sure couldn't count on it staying hidden for much longer, not with patrols out all the time.

"Could be a raid aimed at Naples, either the docks or a terror raid on the rest camp, or maybe a try to stop the supply convoy to Anzio cold, just before they make another push to throw that beachhead back into the sea. What it is really doesn't matter. The point is, it's something big we wouldn't like." He puffed on the pipe again, reflecting. "You did right to call me out, Lieutenant. We need to take some sort of action to make sure that these gentlemen's little private war last night has really shut down whatever the Germans were planning.

"So the next question is, what are they going to do now that they don't have it? They could just as easily be guided by a couple of big bonfires, or for that matter, if they risked coming over in the daytime, they could even use white paint on the ground."

He took another long pause then. Senneman seemed to have thoughts more often than cats had kittens, and with his pipe and heavy horn-rimmed glasses, he looked more like a professor of history or classics than an OSS agent.

"You're thinking," Dan said slowly, "that since they could have done that anyway, if all they needed was something to guide the bombers, then probably this doesn't have anything to do with a bombing raid."

Senneman looked up sharply, over the tops of his glasses. "Aside from being a pretty observant fellow, you apparently read minds. Yes, that's exactly it. I've been jumping to conclusions, and in fact we don't really have enough to go on just yet. What we really should do is get more information, but I would not expect that we can get it from the same site. Either it is out of commission for good, in which case they will have blown up whatever hadn't been destroyed already and pulled out completely, or it is being rebuilt right now, probably ringed with troops. So that's the last place to go back to." He made a little flapping noise with his lips, like a horse. "But still, I have no idea where else we could even think of looking."

Dan had been ransacking through Jackson Houston's memories, and now he had something. "If I had to pick anywhere," he said, "I'd go check at Count Cabrini's. First of all, he's got the biggest house in the area and a private road that leads down to within a few miles of Highway Seven, over on the German side. So if you're right about the big landowners being pro-German, then he's as likely as anyone.

"And there's another good reason, too," he added before they could stop him. He swallowed his fear for his newly improved reputation, and shared the information. "Cabrini is the center of the black market in this whole area. Everything you can think of moves across the lines through his house, one mule load at a time. He's got connections that stretch from Paris to Sicily—the Mafia, the Union Corse, the Paris gangs, they all route it through him.

"So if he isn't working for them, if he didn't get that station put up here, he sure as hell knows something about it. He has eyes and ears everywhere."

There was a long pause, and then Senneman asked quietly, "And how do you know so much about Cabrini?"

"Till not too long ago, I was a pretty big black marketeer myself," Dan said bluntly. "You're always trying to meet your supplier's supplier, to cut the middle out. After a while I found out I was always trying to meet the same guy."

Senneman nodded quietly and sucked on his pipe again. Turenne and the lieutenant seemed a little embarrassed, as if Jackson Houston's activities weren't known to everyone. It took Samson a moment to realize that this was like mentioning a scandal outside the family.

After a long, awkward moment, Senneman said, "It may be of some interest that Count Cabrini is also one of the major backers of the partisans in the area. And we've heard nothing from that source. Which means either Cabrini somehow never noticed that seventy-five or a hundred Germans were setting up that radar base...possible but not likely...or he did know and did not pass the information along. What that implies concerns me a great deal.

"How far off is his house?" Senneman asked.

"You're not planning to just walk up to it?" Flenstein asked. "In the first place he's very big on warning everyone away from his property, and since he's on our list of people to stay on the good side of, we've been careful. But even so he gets jumpy at any kind of visitors. And if he's what you think, he's not going to stop short of killing you."

"If he is, he's also not going to tell me much if he suspects I'm going to seize his house with troops. He might let something slip if it's just me." Senneman stood, dusted the seat of his trousers, straightened his jacket and seemed in general to be making sure he would make the right impression.

"Could you take one or two escorts?" Dan said. "I'd go. At least it's a guide on the way, and one more gun if you need one."

Turenne smiled. "And I think it's a good idea to keep this—what is the expression—'all in the family.' Private Houston already knows everything, so we compromise no information by taking him along. That makes the logical person to do the job either me or Lieutenant Flenstein—and the lieutenant has his men to look after."

Flenstein snorted. "Colonel, that was a very graceful way to send yourself on that mission, but what exactly is the reason for it? You sound to me like you've got something of your own going here.''

Turenne stood and nodded. ''I do. And it's very simple, my friends. I despise collaborators. Some of you may recall that General de Gaulle was *not* the elected president of France, nor even in the upper ranks of the army. And you might remember that in London you can find the Polish government in exile, and the Norwegian, and the Dutch, and on and on, but there is no French government in exile. Our leaders, our generals, decided to stay home and deal with Hitler, to join this Vichy regime. There are those of us who think they sold the country out before, as well, because they were more afraid of losing the next election to their fellow Frenchmen, or of the French labor unions, than they were of bringing the whole country under the German heel. And for men like that—for Pétain, and Laval and their thousands of followers—there should be only the rope, because when we march back into Paris, they will be standing in the balconies, throwing flowers, singing 'La Marseillaise,' and planning to continue running the country now that the Free French have won it back for them.'' The icy contempt in the colonel's voice was something Dan had not heard before. ''So, just possibly, this Cabrini is a collaborator? Then I want to get near him. Very near him.''

Senneman smiled back at him, and there was ice in that smile, as well. ''You are more than welcome,

Colonel." He turned to Dan and said, "My drop kit is still packed. Are you ready to start?"

"In five, Mr. Senneman."

"Can we get there by evening?"

"No sweat, sir. But we may have to camp coming back." Dan sprinted for his pack to throw his few possessions in that were not already packed.

"Geez, since when are you the hero type, Houston?" Quentin, the big red-haired Bostonian, demanded.

"Shit happens," he said, giving the basic answer he would have in his own time.

"I guess so. Who's the guy they dropped to us?"

"Whoever the lieutenant says he is."

Quentin grinned. "Boy, there's a regulation answer. You going to start bringing boot polish and an extra toothbrush on these long-range patrols, too?"

Dan, securing the last of his things, shouldered his pack and lifted his rifle. He smiled at Quentin. "If I do, I'll be sure to let you know. What would you be willing to pay for the brush and the boot polish?"

Quentin laughed. "Now I feel better. I thought the world was ending for a while there." Then suddenly he got more serious and, looking away with embarrassment, he said, "You take care of yourself, okay? We really don't want to have to dig a grave for you in this frozen shit."

Some strange impulse made Dan say, "Naw, don't worry. I'm the one guy you can be sure you won't have to dig a grave for.'' Realizing how odd that must sound, he added, ''The devil isn't about to have anyone muscling in on under-the-table sulfur-and-brimstone action.''

Quentin clapped him on the shoulder and walked away. Dan's researches of his memory showed that Jackson Houston had just had one of his longest friendly conversations with any of Second Platoon since he'd joined them.

In ten more minutes the three of them were over the ridge top, walking at a brisk clip, and their camp was out of sight behind them. Clouds were blowing in over the sun, and it was turning dark and gray out, like a film going from old, time-paled Technicolor to sepia monochrome.

7

The sun was setting as they looked up the road into Cabrini's estate. The big house was a bewildering tangle of white stucco boxes and slopes of red roof, broken by doors and archways apparently at random. As if stuck on to the front, a gallery of columns sheltered what was apparently the front door.

"So, what's the approach?" Dan said. "Ring his bell and shout 'Western Union'?"

"Still too complex," Senneman said. "No, we are simply going to walk up there and knock. Then we will go inside and see if he's willing to say anything. If it gets ugly, we will get away somehow. If we don't get away, then Lieutenant Flenstein will be calling for some help within a day or two, when we don't return."

"That won't do us much good," Dan pointed out.

"Then, *mes amis,* we had best not get captured. Let alone killed. Well, if we are going to walk up there and do this, it may as well be now, before we catch cold." Turenne began the slow walk up the winding half mile of road to the house, and Senneman and Daniel Samson fell into step with him.

Dan knew they were probably in somebody's rifle sights and tried to ignore knowing it. Combat was one thing—sure, you were scared, worse than anyone who hadn't been there could believe, but usually you were busy, too. Walking up to a door that could theoretically have a German machine gun sitting behind it or into a house where fifty Germans might be waiting to dive on them was quite another thing. Supposedly the Germans hadn't been as vicious as the Cong about interrogation, but leave it to Dan Samson's luck to find one who was really creative....

He was frightening himself, he realized, and since he already knew that his situation was dangerous, it was time to stop listening to his fear. Fear is an old friend, but like most old friends, he only talks about one subject and it's hard to get him to shut up about it, he thought, trying to make light of it. It didn't seem very funny, and it didn't make him feel any better.

The sun was down completely now, and the clouds had come over. They managed to stay on the road mostly by how it felt under their boots and by occasional glimpses of the house and outbuildings when some light escaped through painted or curtained windows, or where for just a moment some stable hand needed a lamp or a kitchen girl lit a candle in the outhouse. Once, very briefly, a window lighted brightly and evenly as an electric light came on for a few seconds. The place had to have its own generators.

Somewhere—he wasn't sure if it was Houston's memory, or Samson's—he recalled a phrase from the beginning of this war or had it been World War I? "The lights are going out all across Europe." In a modern war that was exactly what happened. No one was so isolated that a steady gleam, visible from the air, might not bring death raining down.

It was cold, too, and the hastily gobbled K ration of two hours ago was not much antidote either for cold or hunger. As the air began to sting his nose hairs and cool the sweat of his long, strenuous walk, he began to hope that maybe Cabrini would turn out to be all right. They might get a meal out of it, at least.

At last, after having stumbled several times and fallen headlong over potholes or rocks in the road at least once, they stood bruised, cold and tired in front of Cabrini's home. Beside him, almost invisible in the dark, Dan could feel Senneman straightening his uniform as if he were going in to nothing more frightening than a dinner party.

Reflexively Dan bent to knock dirt from the knees of his pants and to snug his jacket down. He realized, after doing it, that the very normality of the action had made him feel a little better.

Senneman stepped forward—Dan felt him vanish from beside him, rather than saw him move to the door—and banged on the door. The hollow thumps seemed impossibly loud after the hours of winter stillness.

For about four long, slow, teeth-numbing breaths, there was no sound or sign of any response. Then there was a little glow, instantly masked, from a window off to the side, and the sound of something sliding back. Dan straightened to look his best.

A light flashed on their faces, very brightly, from up above. It was a little porch light, not much different from what must even then have been over the front doors of a million suburban homes back in America. Dan had been startled, thinking at first that it was a spotlight, not realizing how accustomed to the dark his eyes had grown. Relieved, he looked down to the welcoming door, only to find that it was closed. As he looked, the tiny slide panel that had revealed one eye of indeterminate sex, slid closed.

The light went out.

There were soft footsteps, not returning to whence they had come but apparently going upstairs and fading out as they rose.

It felt as though a couple of centuries went by.

Up above them, at a landing, there was another flare of light, and then the heavy tread of more than one man's boots on the stairs. At last the door really opened and revealed Cabrini, still dressed as if he had just come from a day's grouse shooting, blinking and holding a glass of wine. "I think you had better come in quickly," he said. "I'm afraid the aviators of both sides, out in this empty country, have a habit of attacking any light they can see from the sky."

They entered slowly, finding themselves surrounded by big, burly, rough men, men who wore heavy boots. Each of them held something—a walking stick, a brass candelabra, a fireplace poker—that might have been a weapon, or might have been something he just happened to be holding when he went to see who was at the door.

Cabrini led them down the hall to a small study. The room was slightly shabby but ornate. The rows of books and copies of sculptures suggested that this was a room intended to impress the neighbors, most especially those neighbors who were illiterate peasants, and perhaps to stop the condescension of sophisticated relatives who lived closer to town.

When the other men had departed, Cabrini offered them coffee. Dan felt a little suspicious but realized that nothing would be more of a giveaway than to refuse food and drink, and surely Cabrini, even if he was an Axis agent, would not try poison or drugs while there was still a chance to bluff instead.

Besides, coffee had never tasted better than it did after two straight days of hard work in the icy wasteland outside. Usually, he found from his past incarnation's memories, there was nothing hot to be had for the two weeks of a patrol.

"Now, what can I do for the Allies this evening, Mr., er, I don't believe we've met."

"Robert Senneman. Let me just explain to you that something very strange happened last night. A scouting party found something very odd...."

He described it in a few brief details, leaving out that it had been a radar installation, creating the impression

SOAR WITH THE EAGLE!

And in 1992, the Eagle flies even higher with more gripping adventure reading.

Introducing four new exciting miniseries that deliver action and adventure at a fast pace....

that it had been raided by a party of at least ten men, and making it sound as if they weren't clear on how much damage had actually been done. Dan felt a certain admiration. If for some reason it was ever necessary to tell the truth about anything, Senneman could easily claim that Cabrini had simply misunderstood him. Senneman would have had no problem working for Honest John.

"Just where was this place?" Cabrini asked as he poured everyone a third cup of coffee.

Senneman recited carefully the description provided by Turenne and Dan, omitting the fact that the two of them were the raiding party. Listening to him, Dan noted that he didn't even glance sideways for a confirmation, and yet he was letter-perfect.

When he had finished, Cabrini stood straight up and banged the mantelpiece with his fist. The low fire inside flickered as if he had somehow hit it, as well.

"And on my land! That's been in the family since my great-grandfather's time!"

"Do you know how they would have transported things up there?" Senneman asked.

"Of course. There's an old cattle drover's road up there. The ground is still scraped and bare or trampled flat, nothing grows on it. Not enough dirt to make real mud, so even at this season, once one gets up out of the valleys, there is nothing at all to getting loads of material up it. The reason that the two armies are not fighting here, even at this moment, is that that good road begins in a thick swamp and ends on the edge of a lake, after it visits this house, and it is no more than eight feet wide for much of its length. But it is quite passable, for all that it is slow and could accommodate very little traffic, if one can get to it in the first place.''

''So, if the Germans have thrown a pontoon bridge across in the swamp, then they could have a route into this country.''

''I suppose that is possible.'' Cabrini smiled and refilled the coffee cups without asking, which was fine with Dan. ''The biggest problem they would face, my dear fellow, is that one wrecked lorry would block it. So they could not support a force of any size up here. They might get a few saboteurs or terrorists, that sort of thing, through, I suppose, but I really think that is the limit of what could be done. It sounds as though they had to conceal that base very carefully indeed, and it was quite small.

''These damned silly partisans are suspicious of any nobility or wealth, I'm afraid. It's simply not possible to persuade them that every man with money is not a fascist at heart. They tell me nothing, and none of it gets relayed to you—for surely they must have known more than a little of all this. Well, I shall speak sternly, yes, very sternly, to their captain the next time he visits here.''

He clapped his hands firmly together. ''Now, one custom of the countryside, which I delight in because it so offends my cousins in Rome, is to dine at the reasonable hour of six o'clock and not wait until ten or later, when one is famished, to eat a great heavy bowl of pasta. I would be delighted if you would join me.''

Turenne and Dan glanced at Senneman. He nodded. ''We would be very grateful for your hospitality. Of course, later, if the moon is out, we will need to get on the road and rejoin our unit.''

''By all means, sir. But surely an hour of pleasant conversation and some warm food would not go amiss?''

''Not at all.'' Senneman turned to the others and said, ''Unless, of course, the two of you would rather head back to base?''

They shook their heads. Dan wasn't sure what was up, but if Senneman had decided the count was okay, then there was no sense in missing a good meal, and if Senneman was trying to continue the conversation because he was still suspicious, then the two of them should stay at his side.

The dinner would not have been anything special back in a mess hall in the States, and would have been a little poorer and less tasty than normal in the cheap Italian dive around the corner from Dan's apartment almost half a century in the future. It was really just some shreds of meat off some poor scrawny wretch of a chicken stretched out by a sauce made with home-canned tomatoes and some seasonings and dumped over mounds of noddles. But here...here it was hot, and there was enough of it. It was all Dan could do to refrain from gobbling it like an animal.

The conversation was a little bit over Dan's head, although he had paid attention in his few college courses and recognized some names from the philosophy class and others from literature and art history, but on the whole he was not even that interested. It didn't matter. The subject of the conversation was not fighting, or fear, or for that matter unpaid bills and uncollectable benefits. It was pleasant just to listen to it, to eat off a china plate and silverware that he would not have to wash afterward, in the dancing candlelight, in a room made warm by an extra log on the fire.

He felt little danger from Cabrini. The man was so charming and warm, obviously determined to entertain his guests with whatever he had, and had not even looked askance at their carrying their M-1s right in to dinner, leaning them up in the corner.

Finally they consumed the last of the coffee over some light, delicate pastries, and Senneman said, "Well, it's been delightful, but duty is beginning to call, and I think we should probably answer it, however silly its demands seem in good company."

Cabrini smiled at them. "I do wish that in addition to dinner, I might serve you breakfast. I don't suppose there is anything I can say that would induce you to stay the evening?"

"I'm afraid not," Senneman said, wiping his mouth a last time.

"Even if I pointed out that the moon has not shown itself, which means surely a storm is on the way and in any case it will be terribly dark?"

"No, I'm afraid—"

"Even if I were to say to you 'Put your hands up!'?"

With a crash the two doors into the room flew open. Dan turned instinctively toward his M-1, and saw a German soldier, submachine gun at the ready, standing between him and it.

There was a long, long silence. Cabrini began to stand, and Senneman said, "Gentlemen, I made a very serious mistake. I am sorry."

Dan looked at him and saw that he was pale but calm. Beside him, he knew that Turenne, like himself, would be looking furiously for some way out of their predicament.

There seemed to be none. In minutes their hands were bound behind their backs, and they were being led down into the immense wine cellar of the old house, thirty-five feet or more down a wooden stairway from the door to the house. The cellar's walls were carved directly from the rock, and the air was cool and musty smelling. They passed among long rows of wine casks and into a newer passage that showed evidence of a lot of blasting and of some shaping of the walls.

By the flickering candles they made their way down to the end of the passage to a steel door set into a rough concrete wall. Cabrini smiled as he opened the door, and said, "You know, Mr. Senneman, to be the one

who first sees what is in here . . . that would be the cul-
minating moment in the career of a spy. You really must
congratulate yourself, my dear fellow.''

They entered the place, struggling with their hands
bound behind their backs to get over the high concrete
sill without falling. They saw that it was a prefabri-
cated building, the kind that had popped up all over the
world as the war ebbed and flowed, buried here in a
great, blasted-out cavern. The concrete under their feet
abruptly gave way to rugging over straw mats. Again
they came into dry warmth, a comfortable place. They
went in the second door along the short hallway and
found themselves in a big, bare room with a mirror.

The soldiers filing in behind them closed ranks tightly
around them. They were utterly helpless.

''Well,'' Cabrini said, ''Now our little party will really have something to talk about. It is extremely pleasant to be here with cultivated men such as yourselves,
men who can appreciate the long view of history, men
who can face death with a certain philosophical per-
spective, hard won from much good reading and much
good thinking.

''But perhaps I should not have mentioned death.
After all, although we are all going to die, its immi-
nence, especially when one is still quite young and vig-
orous—well, that is a matter for deep concern, and it
may make you too anxious to properly appreciate the
rest of our conversation.

"So let me first reassure you. The end is not yet, gentle sirs. You are mortal like all men, and so will eventually die, but not just now...."

Cabrini turned and flipped a switch. Suddenly they could see through the mirror, and Dan realized it was a simple one-way viewing setup, not unlike those used in university psychology laboratories in his own time. It allowed people or animals to be watched without their knowing that they had an audience. The bright light on the mirrored glass on the other side effectively turned it into a mirror, while the dimmer light in here made it a window.

As they watched, a dog was led into the room by a bored-looking guard, who clearly had been through this a few times before. It was a starved, mangy mutt that seemed to lick everything around itself as if hoping something would taste good enough to eat. After a few kicks and a yelp or two, the guard succeeded in dragging the pathetic animal, which never stopped wagging its tail, over to a clip on the wall, and attached it there by a short lead from its collar.

The dog yipped frantically when the guard left for a moment. Clearly it wanted to be around people. Probably, Dan thought, it was someone's pet. The quickest way to acquire lab animals up here was probably to just wave a piece of bacon in any village. Hell, in these starved war years, you could probably get some of the villagers that way.

The thought made his blood freeze. He had meant it as a joke to himself, but the moment he thought it, he saw that the metal chairs were bolted down and fitted with shackles. There were stains on the chairs, and especially on the shackles, that were rusted and brown-red in the light. He was suddenly quite sure that Cabrini had tested whatever he had here on more than dogs.

The guard returned, carrying a glass bottle. He seemed to pay much more attention to the bottle than he had paid to the dog. Delicately he set it on a little square object, about the size and shape of a coaster, on top of a small folding metal table. Wires from the "coaster" were connected to two small plugs in the wall. The soldier looked it all over, evidently found it satisfactory and went out. The big "steering wheel" handle on the door spun swiftly. That meant a pressure seal of some kind, Dan figured.

"It is truly not necessary to seal the inner lock on that room, by the way," Cabrini said. "Despite our being so far from the comforts of civilization, our isolation, safety and hazardous chemical facilities are in fact fully as advanced as anything I have seen at the Max Planck Institute in Berlin, or at the IG Farben facilities that your Standard Oil Company was so generous in building for us before the war."

He paused, looking at his captives with an expectant, sly smile. "Now, why should we need such advanced equipment?"

Dan knew it was stupid, but he was getting very tired of the lecture, and besides, he didn't like having everything running on Cabrini's schedule. "Look, if you're going to gas that poor dog just to show us you have poison gas, you can spare us the whole production."

Cabrini roared with laughter, a big, belly-shaking laugh that at first seemed jolly, then grew stranger and stranger as he seemed unable to stop even the tears of pure joy that streaked down his face. He walked up to Daniel Samson and, to his utter disgust, pinched his cheek. "You are so perfect. You are the ideal foil for this." He turned to look at where all the soldiers stood impassively. "I think there are points of interest that you will not have seen before. Throw the switch."

With a bang muffled by the glass wall, the little piece of explosive under the bottle went off, and the greasy, heavy liquid inside—Dan's first thought had been that it was salad oil—vaporized. He saw the dog jump in surprise.

Then it convulsed, its muscles contracting impossibly hard, beyond any control of its will. Its teeth were bared, the breath came out in one shriek and the legs splayed out madly, bones breaking under the force of the contractions. In an instant it was a mere dog-skin rag covering pulped flesh and bone.

"Need I add that this is the effect of a many-times-lethal dose? Even one one-hundredth-thousandth of this dog's exposure would produce essentially the same effect, though less dramatically.

"You are probably familiar with older weapons from your training, and no doubt, thanks to all the peace propaganda of the past decades, you know the effects of older agents like mustard gas or phosgene. And no doubt you realize that this is something quite new.

"The substance you are seeing is called sarin. I am no more supposed to know about it than you are."

Cabrini clapped his hands, and an armchair was carried in. He sat, lit a cigar, smiled at them warmly. "You know, the circumstances of this bring me such deep pleasure. My men here are fierce, loyal fellows, the very best of soldiers. The sort of men who have had trouble elsewhere in the Wehrmacht and have not risen as they deserved to, men who have gotten into trouble with those women-in-pants like Kesselring, Rommel or Guderian because of the old-fashioned Prussian-officer morality. Yes, I dare speak badly of the men I nominally take orders from. Does that surprise you in a German?" He leaned back and lazily blew a smoke ring into the air.

"Oh, and yes, I am quite German. At the end of the last war, as the Western front collapsed, as the Jews and Communists who had infiltrated our navy refused to sail... there were generals with vision. Generals who knew that something was bound to rise again in Germany, from the veterans groups or the industrialists or even the Communists themselves. And so, word went out to a few of us, who were working in the Allied countries, those who had been clever or lucky enough not to get caught, to stay in place. You must understand that in 1919, no one had any idea we could hope for a Mussolini here. But we were told to work for whatever might help Germany once she was able to rise again—and once we had dealt with the traitors that the Versailles treaty put in power.

"So I persevered in my present position, and yet, as I read between the lines, it seemed to me that there were clear indications that things were not going well. The affair at Stalingrad cost us far more than was being officially acknowledged. Manifestly, as Rommel was rolled back from El Alamein, another hope was slipping from our grasp. And so I began to call in old debts, for it was clear to me that Hitler had compromised far too much.

"Through my friends I learned of this marvelous stuff, sarin, and the long-range rockets they are now building. Putting two and two together, I perceived that if twenty tons of sarin—and we already have far more than that in stockpile—could be distributed over southeast England, not only could we kill everyone in London, but we could also finish off the air forces that now bomb Germany, the invasion army wherever it might be. In one night we could erase all the preparations you and the British and your pet Frenchmen have made since Dunkerque.

"Those long-range rockets carry a bit under a ton of payload each. Twenty-five rockets to stop the invasion cold, without our even having to find the precise place to target, and to fill London with a few million fresh corpses in the bargain. Perhaps ten more tons of sarin to roll your forces back out of Italy. It might take as much as fifty to reverse the direction of the Eastern Front, with another ten delivered by rocket to Moscow, thereby ridding us of those tiresome Bolshevik donkeys.

"Now, that might buy us a year, and there are plans already on the drawing board for the next step—the rockets that can be launched from U-boats, the rockets that can cross the Atlantic in thirty minutes. If Roosevelt sees reason and makes peace, getting Russia and Britain out of the war, he might get two full years before we resume with the eradication program. For starters, Washington D.C., world capital of the Freemasons, and then, Jew York and Jew Jersey? In a single night.

"Do you see? Do you understand? Fewer men than those who held you at the Rapido a month ago could win us the war, and the world, by 1948."

Suppose that happens, Dan thought. The Bomb had come along in what, summer of '45? And as far as he could remember, it had been built in Tennessee, New Mexico, somewhere up in Washington State...no, they weren't going to win this one. Not even with nerve gas in V2s. It was already too late. But how many more millions dead would it take? How many more years would the death camps run before Berlin disappeared under the mushroom cloud?

"We have some thousands of tons of sarin already, and we could make more. And the long-range rockets will be ready soon enough.

"But I regret to report that our high command is made up almost entirely of timid men. And those few with the imagination and will probably do not even know of both these innovations. The burdens of wartime secrecy, you know. So they could not launch the attack, out of ignorance, even if they did have the courage."

Courage, Dan thought. That was a word he'd heard too much since he got back from Nam, always from people who talked about the courage to take certain measures or set policies. They did not mean the plain courage, the facing of fear and danger, that the three bound men, or Lieutenant Flenstein and his men, or all the ordinary fighting men in Vietnam, had lived by. They meant the courage to strangle your own conscience and do what you damned well knew was wrong. The Nazi kind of courage. Had it started back here? Or was it somewhere else?

He knew deep inside, in the places that had awakened in the Wind Between Time, that he was very close now to what he had to accomplish... that he had almost discovered what the fight was about and why he was here in the time stream.

But now Cabrini was up, pacing, waving his arms excitedly. "And yet high command will delay and dither and fret away our chance of victory... unless they become truly committed to it. But once sarin has been used, they will see that the only alternative is to use more of it. If the invasion can be delayed just a few months or even a few weeks, the rockets are almost ready to fly.

"It so happens I have a few tons of sarin of my own, and better still, I have received, courtesy of some friends at Peenemünde, a collection of experimental rockets from their early work. Nothing to carry a ton of material six hundred miles, you understand, but Italy is only a hundred miles wide, and I am very nearly at the center. The sixty miles that these rockets can travel and the fifty pounds they can carry will do very nicely.

"From here I can strike at your forward positions at Ortona in the east, your great massings of force preparing to strike again at Monte Cassino, and even at the major rear staging area in Naples. Two trucks, with half a dozen rockets each, less than a day later, will clear the beachhead at Anzio and wipe out the crews of a thousand bombers at Foggia—the rockets need only get twenty miles closer for either of those targets.

"There remains but one truck convoy, due in a few hours, and I shall be able to begin readying the rockets.

"You can take some pride in having inconvenienced me and forced me to spray more gas more indiscriminately. What you destroyed was a tracking station that would have let me know where each shot fell so that as soon as I had hit one sector, I could move on and hit the next. I'm afraid that now, instead of using perhaps a third of my rockets, I shall have to use all of them to make sure I get everything, and concentrate more heavily on Naples and Foggia, since those are bigger targets and easier to hit. Still, there will be plenty left over for Monte Cassino. And after all, the added deaths in Naples and Foggia will be mostly civilian, merely Italians, who have already proven themselves thoroughly worthless to both sides."

He faced them, rubbing his hands as though he were getting down to a much anticipated task. "What do you suppose the reaction will be? Tens of thousands of Allied troops dead. The road suddenly open for our men to retake Anzio and to sweep down the west coast to Naples and the east coast to Foggia, if not farther. I know that two full Allied divisions, and many smaller units, have left Italy in the past month to join your upcoming invasion of France. You will lose the better part of twenty-five divisions. How many will have to be pulled out of Britain, back to the Mediterranean? How long before you can reestablish your lines here? And after that, another year, or more, before you can invade.

"But you will not have that year. In a scant couple of months at most, the great attacks will begin on Britain and Russia, and Roosevelt may be asking for peace by Christmas.

"It is for this that the three of you are going to die. Because I shall launch my rockets as soon as I am able, and having told you this, I have made you all dead.

"Because I know you are the sort of men to fully appreciate historical irony, I have decided to use you as my test subjects. Although the sarin we have here was good when it left the base where it was developed and seems to be quite effective on dogs, we do need to make sure it will work on human beings."

He nodded slightly, but his soldiers understood. Three of them grabbed Senneman, who gave a frightened yelp before, with a hard swallow, he composed himself again.

Cabrini seemed very amused. "What is this, a cry of despair? Not quite the brave fellow you thought you would be?" He smiled and said, "Don't worry. It will be over in a little while." He gave an order in German. His feet trailing behind him, no longer bearing his weight, Senneman was dragged off.

"Perhaps we will let our gentlemen be alone here," Cabrini said. "Guards at each door, of course, but let us permit these fine gentlemen the use of their legs and a bit of pleasant conversation. We can observe the experiment from the other window just as well, and I suspect that if we stay here they will only be able to gratify themselves by calling us names."

He left. The soldiers followed, and the door slammed shut.

"He's listening, of course," Dan said.

Turenne nodded. "For all we know, he is recording this so that he can play the record of it over and over again, but at this point, it does not really matter."

Then the lights came on in the other room. The door was flung open, out into an unseen hallway, and they saw part of Senneman's body. The OSS man was kicking and struggling, and he had managed to brace both feet on the door frame. They beat at his legs futilely for a while, then suddenly slapped his crotch. As his legs flew together, the German guards hurled him onto the floor. With his hands bound behind him, he couldn't cushion his fall, and his wrists slammed into his lower spine.

He had not gotten lucky, all the same. His head did not slam hard enough to fracture his skull or give him a concussion, so though he was plainly hurt, one arm perhaps dislocated, he was still quite conscious. He gasped with pain, kicked with his legs, tried to jam himself back into the doorway, but they were on him, lifting him, forcing him down into the chair, wrenching at his injured arm any time he braced himself.

Senneman's face was streaked with tears and blood ran from the corner of his mouth. Dan felt his stomach rising and looked away.

He tried his bonds again. He was still trussed tight. The old Houdini trick of tensing his muscles as he was tied had gotten him a tiny bit of purchase, but no more.

Turenne sighed. "I have carried out executions myself when I was given Legion troops in Algeria, between the wars. Only a rare man makes a good show at his death.''

''What difference can it make?'' Dan whispered.

''Precisely. I meant only that your compatriot is no coward. These are the normal ways a man responds to being killed deliberately and officially.'' Turenne groaned, ''Oh, for God's sake get that over with, you Boche barbarian swine.''

Dan did not answer. He was sinking his concentration deep inside, feeling to see what he might be able to do with the tiny bit of slack he had.

Few ropes bind so tightly that escape is completely impossible, and he had been tied in haste. Slowly he worked a finger, then two, under the top wrap on one wrist. He began to breathe more deeply and slowly as he sank into the deepest sort of concentration. He thought of his hands as burning hot, of his bones as melting like butter, of everything below his shoulders being numb. He found the pain of the rope and leaned into it, leaned against it, focused in the way that a hundred teachers, from Yei Yul Kim forward, had taught him to do in the past twenty years of his life.

As his hands warmed, the capillaries dilating, they began to sweat, at first a little, then profusely. The salt stung the places where the rope had rubbed him raw, but the moisture lubricated his skin and the rope, and it loosened a little and began to creep upward on his hand.

He found the pain and bore down on it, trying to press further still.

A detached part of his mind was still listening, and even watching, as they forced Senneman's hurt arm into the straps on the chair and strapped it down. He had to look as if he was doing nothing, in case there was some way they could observe him, but the dissociation and the deep meditation required to work the ropes switched off much of what he felt. It was only later that he would know the full horror of Senneman's face, blood streaming from the nose and broken teeth where they had hit him, eyes staring wide with terror, the breath a shriek, the face so distorted with tension that had they not known, they could not have recognized him as Senneman.

The rope gave a bit further, lubricated by the blood welling from Samson's scraped skin. The calm, focused part of his mind, the only part he permitted himself to be aware of, acknowledged that in fact he now had a slightly better chance of breaking free, but it did not begin to hope for escape or to fear that he was hurt—it was beyond all that.

Cabrini's voice came to them over some hidden speaker. Dan continued to work on his bonds, but he consciously reminded himself to look up as if startled.

"Now, what we see here is a little demonstration of what can happen with much lower doses."

Senneman was trying to take a big enough windup with the little bit of slack in the cords binding his head, but he couldn't, and instead of knocking himself out, he merely battered the back of his head. It must have hurt like hell, but he kept doing it.

"The technician coming in now . . ."

The figure that opened the door was wearing what looked very much like environment suits Dan had seen. At the end of a long stick, he held a test tube with a stopper. In the test tube gleamed a single oily drop of pure death.

"He is bringing a single drop of about a tenth of a milliliter. This is far more than enough to kill Mr. Senneman very quickly, if directly applied."

Dan felt the loop rise along the base of his little finger, felt the crunching cartilage in each knuckle, and the rope was that much lighter in its grip on him.

The technician gently set the bottle into a rack in the back corner of the room, attached a thin chain, descending from a hook dangling from the ceiling, to the stopper and backed swiftly out of the room. On his way out, he paused a moment to use the stick to whack Senneman's unprotected face, leaving a red welt rising from one cheek. Laughter and applause came over the speaker, drowning out Cabrini's voice for a moment.

"The test to determine how fast a simple drop evaporating in an enclosed volume will actually produce fatality will allow us to calibrate necessary attack intensities . . ."

Dan's ring finger came free, and now he could begin to press to lift the second winding. His wrist slick with

blood and sweat, the rope began to slide easily. All he
had to do was empty his lungs completely, hang in the
airless pain a moment, and now he was two windings
off. He pressed his wrists together and upward, hurting
his shoulders but distributing the slack. A jerk downward, ready to work the rest off. To make sure what he
was doing stayed concealed, he took the space of two
long breaths to feed the coils into the palm of his freer
hand, where he could stretch them farther and have
them ready, if necessary, to slip his hand back through
for concealment.

There was a tiny whining buzz like the sound of a
mosquito on a still night. Turenne, beside Dan, was
speaking very softly and with a perfectly even intona-
tion. "Lord have mercy. Christ have mercy. Lord have
mercy."

The hook began to rise. The chain drew tight.

Senneman's eyes opened wide. He drew a deep
breath, seemed to compose himself and then said, very
loudly, "Don't let the educated accent fool you. I got
that on scholarship at Oxford. My people are from
Brooklyn. My kid brother Sidney's in the Marines
someplace. Tell him he says kaddish for me or I'll haunt
him, and tell all the rest I love them."

There was the soft clink of the glass stopper popping
free of the test tube, and its delicate pinging against the
wall as it swung. The oily little drop of sarin seemed to
smolder, release a thin white strand of evil smoke like a
cobra rising from a snake charmer's basket.

"Note that despite its oily composition the compound is in fact highly volatile," Cabrini's voice said. It sounded so much like a classroom lecture that Dan's mind leaped to a conclusion.

"I think the son of a bitch is filming this," Dan said incredulously.

Somehow that was the one thing that simply snapped him out of the peaceful, calm state he had needed to free himself from his bonds, and into a need to fight and wound and strike and keep on striking, even if they killed him in the first second. The thought of Robert Senneman's death agony, preserved to amuse his Nazi tormentors, or to be pored over by soulless scientists trying to improve this foul insecticide for people, was simply too much. That Cabrini had spoken English rather than German, to be sure Senneman would understand all the words up to the last instant and to try to leave his comrades with a humiliating memory of him . . . this only added fuel to the fire.

The rest of the sarin vaporized with a rush, a puff of light white above the mouth of the test tube, and there was a long, long second before, at first slowly and imperceptibly and then with terrible speed, Robert Senneman tensed in the chair, his lips drawn back in a horrible grin as his teeth clamped together, his flesh pressed into the steel restraints without effect, head arching back until he was looking straight upward, chest contracting for the last time, expelling the last of his air. Perhaps his heart had already stopped.

With a sound like a soggy wet pistol shot, his thigh bones shattered from the force of his muscle contractions, and their jagged ends tore upward out of his pants as both shoulders dislocated from the force of his cramping back muscles.

His own body had simply torn itself to pieces.

"Three-point-eight seconds in a volume of six cubic meters," Cabrini said, his voice showing its deep pleasure but staying carefully level so that whoever was to use the film would have the necessary information.

The hate that swelled in Daniel Samson then was deep and hot. He thought for a long, terrible moment that he wanted Cabrini's grim plan to succeed, because he knew that the losses from gas would be avenged with the Bomb. Hadn't he read someplace that they were very close to the H-bomb at the end of the war, that Teller was rushing to get it worked out when they canceled it? He pictured New Year's Day of 1946, a great crater like the mouth of a roaring devil opening where Berlin had been, a hundred mushrooms sprouting from German soil, the air rich with the rain of vaporized Germans....

An icy hand squeezed its frozen fingers into his brain. How many innocent dead to satisfy his rage? For how many years had he learned to keep his head when a fight was imminent?

He was calm again. More than that, he was deeply cold inside. Sometime soon he would thaw out the fresh wound of Senneman's death, let it bleed itself clean. For now, to live through this at all would be the only possible sort of revenge.

8

After they had vented the sarin-contaminated room, they seemed to take a very long time to get back to Dan and Turenne. As they sat waiting, Turenne asked casually, "What is kaddish? I know Senneman was an old, close friend of yours...." His foot moved close to Samson's, as if to comfort him.

Dan was a bit startled, but maybe a French officer just wouldn't know, so he said, "It's a prayer for the dead. His family is obligated to say it for a year...."

Turenne's foot was scraping his leg in a simple, regular pattern. He reached back into Jackson Houston's memories, and recognized suddenly that this was Morse code.

"My...hands...are...free," Turenne signaled.

"Mine R 2," Dan tapped back as he kept frantically talking about kaddish, high holy days and anything that vaguely seemed as though it might be on the topic.

"Go when they come or wait?"

That took Turenne a long time to tap out. Dan's reply was simpler.

"Now."

"Ok."

Dan shrugged the rope off his hands. Turenne's fell away in ribbons, as if slashed. A moment later, confirming this, Turenne handed him a small, sharp knife. Dan was about to gesture, protesting that he couldn't take Turenne's weapon, when the Frenchman produced two more knives from his sleeves, one for each of his hands.

Dan suspected you got habits like that in the Maquis, and the guards had certainly searched them carelessly.

He looked the situation over. Two doors were guarded, but only one that they knew about was connected to a passageway leading to the outside. Probably Cabrini and his men were either still over where they had been watching the fun—just two doors down—or else something had come up.

Or maybe they were just watching on a hidden camera and laughing.

Part of his mind leaped with pleasure. This was the forties. Probably no hidden cameras, unless they could afford the time to have film developed. The only other observation posts might be one-way glass—and the window to the test room was the only glass in the room—or maybe a peephole somewhere. But as he scanned, he saw no evidence of one. Probably they thought the mike was enough, or more likely the mike had to be enough because that was all there was.

Sometimes the best tactics were the simplest. Dan turned and beat on the door through which they had been tossed into the little room, pounding with his bloody fists. Then he turned off the light and moved to the side of the door to wait for developments.

Sure enough a guard opened the door a little and, seeing nothing, reached in to flick the light switch.

Dan grasped the wrist, taking up the slack of the guard's arm in one smooth stroke toward the hand, and drew him forward, letting his free hand, the knife held out, slide up the guard's arm. The guard had only time to gasp and grunt with surprise before Dan's knuckles reached his shoulder and the razor-sharp edge of the knife struck suddenly across, slashing his throat from ear to ear.

Dan dragged the body inside. Turenne moved to the door and cautiously pulled it open.

In a moment they were out in the corridor and headed back toward the door for the outside world. For an instant Dan thought they might get a clean break, but the hope was dashed with a sudden loud outcry behind him. Whatever their captors had been doing in that other room, they had finished and emerged just in time to see the open door and the two men's backs.

A pistol shot rang off the steel overhead. Officers' pistols were obviously just as useless as they'd ever been. From the way they were shouting at the one who had fired, apparently there was a real risk of accidentally releasing the sarin here. Dan seriously doubted that anything else would have put that hysterical note into their voices.

Another turn brought them to the steel door. Their pursuers were not more than fifty feet behind them, but Dan took a moment to grab an electric cord, drop a loop of it around the door handle and, after pulling it shut, snug it tight to one of the support pillars, thus holding the inward-swinging door closed.

"Good trick," Turenne noted. That was the only word they exchanged as they fled around the winding passage and on up into the wine cellar.

On the steps leading to the main house were several of the "peasants" and "servants." Luckily they either were not trusted enough to have guns or had not found them to get them.

Turenne, in the lead, pivoted, broke the first man's knee with a kick, slashed his forehead to blind him with blood on his way down and stamped on his hand to make him drop the stick he held. Dan slipped in next to the wall and cross-braced with his wrists to stop the stick whistling down.

Before he could deliver his next blow, Turenne had spun on the ball of his foot, jammed a hard kick under the man's jaw and slashed his exposed belly.

The men with the clubs were plainly ordinary soldiers. They were used to a rifle, and brave enough to stand by a gun, but direct face-to-face, flesh-to-flesh combat was almost outside their training and experience. Most of them swung their clubs overhand in big, open arcs that deflected easily to the side, leaving their torsos unguarded. Only one had sense enough to use a short stick as a jabbing implement, and since Dan and Turenne had him flanked, the worst injury the two sustained was a couple of glancing blows to shoulders and upper arms.

They might have been trapped at the top of the stairs. Although the narrow stairs allowed only one man fighting room, at the head of the stairs five men with clubs, or even with broom handles, could have held them long enough for their pursuers to catch up, for from the sounds behind it was clear that their pursuers had managed at last to open the door.

But frightened as they were by the two men's efficient, apparently inexorable progression up the stairs, they broke and ran when a simple retreat to the head of the stairs would have finished off Dan and Turenne.

The two rushed, gained their stair head, and were in the main body of the house.

"They may be going for guns," Turenne said. "We should hurry."

They raced down the hall, boots booming on the wooden floor, looking for any obvious exit. The study opened to their left, and now they knew where they were. Had they really sat chatting here with Senneman and the count just two short hours before? A kerosene lantern still burned dimly on the table, and the hearth still glowed.

With a single motion, Turenne scooped up the lantern, pivoted and kicked the largest of the standing bookcases, spilling it toward the fireplace in a great cascade of open books, and pitched the lantern with all his might against the back wall of the fireplace.

The lantern shattered instantly. Kerosene sprayed back onto the great pile of books, and the lantern itself plus the hearth sent it all up in flames.

Turenne grabbed Dan's elbow. "Let's run!"

They took off at full speed. It was not till they had knocked down a slow-moving but very large man and gotten through the front door, and then were safely over the ridge line after a running stumble of skinned hands and knees, that they slowed to a pace where conversation was possible. The moon had begun to pop in and out of the clouds, and by this intermittent light they made good quick time, but behind them they could hear a search organizing.

"Where did you learn the trick with the cord?" Turenne asked as they trotted through the mud and slush, getting distance between themselves and the foe.

"In a fraternity house, sir," Dan said, hoping the explanation would satisfy the colonel. It was also true. "And, if I can ask, Colonel, what kind of fighting technique is that? And why did you stop to burn his library?"

Turenne panted for a moment as they topped the shadowed part of a ridge. "Ha. Not as young as I once was. So hard to do a run like this three days in a row. Well, *mon ami,* in the command of Legion troops one learns a few things. That is simply the more savage form of savate, the way it was first developed by criminals—

along with the little trick of always carrying a few common kitchen knives about oneself, attached with adhesive tape, because there is not always time for a search to be thorough. It helps, too, to be in the habit of wearing steel-toed boots, just as so many of the Parisian criminals do.''

They turned uphill, and there was no breath for conversation. Here, in the shadow of the ridge, it was pitch-black, and though it would surely conceal them, they could easily turn an ankle or fall headlong at any moment.

They rolled low over a dark spot on the ridge line, and then scampered quickly down into the little ravine to get off the brightly moonlit slope, their boots scraping and thumping.

As they moved up the ravine, now more cautiously, Turenne added, ''And as for burning his library—faugh! Any man who can hold opinions like that on the Russian novelists cannot have read them, even if he has passed his eyes over them. And what loss to the world is a book where there is no one to read? It merely removed an absurdity.''

They came to the head of the ravine, where a few tall, thick pines created shadows in which they could stand and look out over the broken country around them. The barren desolation was almost beautiful in the silver of the moon. You could forget that the cruel earth, only six inches deep, was starving everyone who lived here, that all the white patches were products of snowstorms that could kill an exposed man in thirty minutes. There was just the deep silence of the open sky, with stars like burning steel in the dark holes in the moonlit clouds. The blue-gray land stretching in all directions to the heavy, dark shadows of the mountains looked as if no one had ever touched it.

As they watched, lights flared briefly in the direction from where they had come, then were swallowed up by the night.

"Checking for tracks, probably," Dan said. "But they aren't looking anywhere we've been, either going in or coming out. From what Cabrini said, it sounds like they are really just waiting for the last truckloads of fuel. And I hate to say this, but much as we set them back with destroying their tracking center, all he really has to do is get a few lucky shots and he's home free."

"Then we must see he does not get them. Do you know this country, Houston?"

Dan looked around and researched the memories. "I think so. We need to head toward that peak, if I'm right, and if I'm not, it's no worse than any other direction. I guess we'd better hurry—I'd hate to see history change because we ran out of breath."

Turenne laughed. "'History is a marathon whose finish line we struggle to reach.' We will make a philosopher of you yet, my American gangster."

As they jogged on, it occurred to Dan that he couldn't ask for better circumstances, given the situation: a good officer to follow, a long road to run, and the moon to light his way.

9

In twenty-five minutes they had found camp. As difficult as it was in the night, Dan had ranged the country as a scout for the long-range patrols, and he had learned to find his way almost anywhere within two or three miles of the main patrol route. Moreover, Turenne's sense of direction was good, and he was attentive in wild country. The hardest thing to teach, and the most important, in finding your way without a trail, is to pay attention to the right things.

More time with the Legion, or the Maquis, or God knows what, Dan thought. Along the way he had learned that Turenne's usual command was in a Moroccan brigade—wild mountaineers from the roughest, most remote corner of France's North African empire. He would have been willing to bet that they bragged to other outfits about what a tough bugger their CO was.

As they topped the ridge, Dan quietly clapped out the arranged rhythm to let them know it was not the enemy. Flenstein's men were too good to have sentries easily seen, but Dan figured that somewhere up in those cold rocks there were undoubtedly at least four rifles trained on them.

He didn't really know for sure, but twenty seconds after giving the signal, Quentin was standing at his elbow, tilting his chin up to check his face in the moonlight. A moment later Turenne, too, was approved, and they were guided into the camp.

When they joined Flenstein, he was wide-awake. "We had a little clash with a German patrol just at sunset. Nobody hurt on either side, and we drove them off, but by then it was so dark there was no hope of breaking camp and moving, so we had to get a lot of guards out and just kind of hope that nothing tougher turns up. Probably by now nothing's moving anyway."

Turenne sighed. "I have all sorts of news for you."

Dan let Turenne do the talking—the man practiced enough, after all, and besides, he had more rank than any of the others. It took a while for him to get the whole idea across, but when he did, Flenstein called Scott over and was giving the basic orders in five minutes.

"Houston, you're going to have to guide the platoon back. We'll take everything we've got. I hate to be responsible for doing it again, but I'm going to break radio silence one more time. The problem is that sometimes it takes an hour to get through. Since we don't have the time to wait around, Sparks will have to see if he can get his precious set working from muleback."

Tech Sergeant Swanson, whom nobody but the lieutenant ever called "Sparks," swore and muttered, but he kept fussing with the gear hanging in one pannier off the side of a mule. "Maybe if we get an extra-long antenna, say, have two guys carry a wire out the back..."

Dan couldn't quite believe that the United States had gotten through a whole war with such delicate, unreliable radios as that one, but as he hurried up to talk to Diangelo, the sergeant in charge of the point squad, he consoled himself with the thought that more rugged, compact ones probably hadn't been available from the Japanese.

Diangelo was a slow, deliberate, imperturbable man who seemed to be trying to undo every stereotype about Italian-Americans all by himself. "Glad to have you, Houston. For once we'll at least have an idea about where we're going. Guys, gather 'round. Private Houston here has been over the ground, I guess twice, recently. And he can tell us something or other about what it is we're going into, I bet...if he's supposed to."

That gave Dan a moment's pause. He'd had no orders at all about secrecy so he simply said, "Well, I don't know officially. A lot of you have met up with Cabrini, and a lot of you don't like him, and it turns out you've been right all along. Colonel Turenne and the guy for OSS found out he's a German agent. I'm not sure I could explain to you what's going on in that house, but the main thing is, they're using it as a base for...uh, long-range weapons...stuff that could hit, say, Naples. So if you don't want your time in rest camp spoiled..."

It was about the stupidest attempt at inspiration he'd ever heard, so Dan quickly got into a discussion of the ground. He had to make heavy use of Jackson Houston's memories to interpret it all, but as he saw the men nodding, asking quietly for clarification—when he saw the respect that the new Private Houston was getting— he didn't think Houston would have minded much.

Or am I Houston? he thought as he started down the slope with the pointman from Diangelo's squad. He had to admit to himself that besides the purely factual information and the skills Houston had, he hadn't made much use of those memories, and what he had found had repelled him—an unending catalog of petty theft and lying, taking whatever he could get any way he could, cheating and whining, and yet...

When Houston had whined, it had been in Samson's voice, and it had been the same way he had whined at his mother as a small child, before she had broken him of it, lovingly and gently but with a will of iron. Just as she had gotten him out of lying, cheating, stealing, and taught him not to take advantage of the weak. His big sister and younger brothers had helped, and his scout-master, and half a dozen teachers he had not thought of in years. Daniel Samson had grown up with not much in the way of material comfort, but a lot of people on his side, people who counted on him to come out right.

The best thing anyone in the Houston family had ever done for little Jackie was to ignore him. Dan could feel that there were plenty of people who could have helped him onto the straight and narrow if he'd wanted to be there, but he wasn't sure Houston would have perceived them.

Even in the Army, if Houston had simply dedicated his talents for deception and stealth to being the good scout he was, he could have been somebody in the unit a lot sooner than this belated, grudging recognition Dan was winning for him.

Well, it didn't really matter. Dan probably did not have time enough to clean up the whole mess of Jackson Houston's life, but he hoped by the time he was done he might have at least put in a few notes of grace.

The platoon was now fully in motion. Compared with what lay ahead of them, neither of his night expeditions with Turenne had been difficult. The fighting had been hard, the distances long, and in this wild country the danger would have been great even without Germans, but nothing compared with the problem of moving forty-five men and thirty fully loaded mules four miles through such terrain in the dead of a winter night. The Houston part of his memories estimated that they would be lucky if they only lost two men to injuries and killed a mule per mile.

To begin with, they had to maintain some kind of formation and be ready to fight at any moment. That meant picking places where at least in theory they could pass in something more than single file, though often enough they had to slow down and do exactly that. The ground seemed to have a maddening habit of getting easy in exactly the direction that would have silhouetted them against the moon. So they were forced to pick dark, broken ground, littered with rocks of every size and punctuated by short cliffs, slides of gravel and deep hollows filled with soft snow into which a man would sink up to his waist, getting drenched to the bone in icy meltwater.

Where one man could simply pick his way, Lieutenant Flenstein had to worry that the vanguard of his platoon might trample the ground to mud and make it too slick and dangerous for the rear. A man by himself could simply come back out of a dead end. A platoon would have to reorient itself so that it would be able to fight in the direction it was moving, at the cost of much precious time. On his own, a man could rely on concealment, and take whatever way was easiest on whatever schedule he could manage. Nothing could hide a whole platoon on the move out in this barren country, and they had to take the route that let them cover each other, even though it might force every one of them onto more difficult ground or make him race to hold position with regard to his mates.

Even now, Dan felt that he had the easy job. All he had to do was go by the widest, most open ways that he could find, avoiding skylines and the deeper parts of ravines. What Lieutenant Flenstein and the rest of the platoon were going through behind him, he preferred not to think about. Yet the only sounds were the occasional scrabbling of boots on gravel as someone lost and

then regained balance, or the involuntary "oomph" of
a man landing on his butt in the mud.

Once there was a loud crash, a deep groan and a bray
that were instantly silenced, but not before he heard
very clearly someone say "Fuck!" A moment later
word was passed up to them that they were to hold position for five minutes. There might have been some
jingling or the sound of struggle out there as they held
down the pack mule, cut its throat, redistributed its load
to the other mules, who were skittish from the smell of
blood, and got back into formation to move. But if Dan
had been scouting for the other side, he really would not
have been sure that those sounds were not just his
imagination.

He'd have been damned glad to have these men with
him on night patrol in Nam or anywhere.

As they waited, he flexed his hands. They were getting sore, and he was sure that in another day or two,
between the scraping they'd had as he escaped and the
horrible cold seeping in through his gloves, he would
have a hell of a time handling the carbine that the unit
had lent him.

"Losing government property," Quentin had said as
he issued the new weapon—one of only four spares the
platoon could afford to carry. "Ain't you got any respect? Tax money paid for that rifle."

Then the word got passed along from the rear, and on
stiff, sore legs, he stood and they began to work their
way forward again. Dan had been point more often

than not in Vietnam, so it irked him a little to have the point twenty yards out in front of him most of the time, but he had to admit that since only he and Turenne knew the ground, and Turenne had to stay back with Flenstein, that left him too valuable to get killed accidentally.

It wasn't so bad for either Jackson Houston or for Daniel Samson to feel valuable, he decided.

They picked their way carefully through the pines on the lee side of a zigzag draw. It was very dark in the shadows, and the cold and damp seemed much more acute, but the snow had melted less, the thick blanket of needles muffled their footsteps, and it simply felt safer. Overhead the stars were impossibly bright. It had been a long time since Dan had been outside a city late at night, and he'd forgotten how bright they were and how many.

There were two hours left till dawn when they finally looked down from a hill across the valley from Cabrini's house. There were no lights on down below, but clearly something or someone was moving around between the buildings.

After a minute or two Lieutenant Flenstein and Turenne came up beside him.

"The good news is that the B-17s are on their way—they're going to pound that place into rubble," Flenstein said. "But they won't get here for three hours. There were a lot of calls for raids this past night, and they've got to get them fueled and loaded with bombs."

"So we've got to keep Cabrini and his men bottled up till then," Turenne said. "Houston, I would like to take you and two other men and see if we can lay an ambush on that road. If what he is waiting for is a truck convoy or a mule train, then delaying that will get us enough time. But if, at this point, you are too tired—"

"I'll come," Dan said. "I couldn't miss out now—it's just beginning to get exciting."

Turenne smiled, but he seemed tired and worn.

"For the rest of it," Flenstein said, "my old buddy from CCNY, Freebie Schwartz, is the guy I got through to at Foggia. According to him, the best thing for the B-17s would be if that building got set on fire—it'll make it a much clearer target. So in about an hour and a half, I'm going to start an attack down the hill and see if we can lob phosphorus grenades through their windows, and see what else we can get burning."

"Watch what you get close to, sir," Dan said, and suddenly realized that it would be very hard to explain how he knew that the fuel was likely to be something like liquid oxygen and kerosene. "Uh, if it can propel a rocket sixty miles . . . it's got to be something—"

"That would blow like hell if we set it off. Good point, Houston. We'll try to keep the men well back from things." Then the lieutenant laughed, a good, open sound that made everyone there feel better. "After all, we don't want to get these fellows involved in anything dangerous."

For the ambush in the road, they chose Quentin, because he was supposed to be good with a BAR, and Sutherland, a small, freckled kid who had worked with explosives a lot and was competent with a mortar. Dan swapped his carbine for a regular M-1, as he was planning to do some sniping, and Turenne got his tommy gun back.

It was a fast trot for almost a mile through that broken country, and there were more bruises for everyone before they got down to the point Turenne had chosen, a place where the road—or more accurately, the cattle track—was pinned between a steep ravine and a spur off a low mountain just at a double bend in the road.

Here the road, headed south, bent sharply to the west, curved back north and then hairpinned back to the south before finally straightening out, all in less than a quarter mile.

Turenne surveyed the site with some satisfaction. "All right, then, we will do this by the book. Houston, take a position in the rocks up there. When the charges knock out the first truck, open up on the truck farthest toward the rear that you can see. Try for the driver or anything that will stop it. After that, whatever you can get that you think will do the most good.

"Quentin, down there, with the BAR, where you can sweep the road. Find a place where you can fire accurately. Try to get fuel tanks, drivers, things like that, and if Houston's guess about the nature of the cargo is accurate, it may be worth putting a few rounds into the cargo of each truck.

"Sutherland, start from the ends and walk mortar fire inward toward the center of the convoy.

"And I shall stay down close. Watch for my hand signals in case some opportunity arises. Since I have no idea how far or how hard this stuff is going to blow up—or if it will—I shall simply pick the best distance for the Thompson gun and hope that that will turn out to have been appropriate.

"And now, gentlemen, the part of the ambush that those of us experienced in the Maquis always most look forward to—we need a hole in the middle of that road, right now. Put all the dirt on a shelter half and mind you don't disturb anything except the place where you make the hole." He grinned at them. "Meanwhile, I shall stand guard. Someone has to, and I have just remembered that I am a colonel."

It was probably a measure of the regard they held him in that they all laughed without feigning.

As Dan grabbed his entrenching tool and pitched in, he noticed that Quentin and Sutherland were just faintly surprised, and realized that once again he was being untypical of Jackson Houston. Well, they could get used to it, no doubt, if they lived through the day.

At a depth of four inches, they were at rock-hard frozen dirt, and further progress with the spades was impossible. Sutherland got the chisels and sledge, and they began to chip out chunks of frozen earth, which broke out in little pieces not much bigger than their fists.

They needed only a hole one foot deep and one foot square for the charge, but it took a full sweaty, grunting, hand-stinging hour to make the hole, and only five minutes to plant and wire the charge, running the wires just barely below the earth. "One consolation in all this," Sutherland said, taking off his helmet to wipe his sweat-soaked hair, panting and hot even though the temperature was still somewhere below freezing. "The earth is so hard that the hole is a perfect reflector. It'll be like having a shaped charge stuck underneath the target. Set that off under a truck, and when that blast reflects straight up out of that hole, it'll clean his clock for dead-solid certain, you bet."

Quentin grinned. "Just so I'm down here low enough to warm my hands at the fire. I'm sweating like a pig, but my nose feels like it's going to freeze off right now."

"Well, *mes ami,* let's see how you've done." Turenne surveyed their work and said, "All right. Two things remain to be done. Pile small stones, no bigger than your fist, all over where the charge is. A pile of rocks is nothing on this road, and it will hide any visible lines. Quentin, you're in charge of that. You other two, grab a log or post from the side of the road and drag it along the wheel ruts there. Start from up by the bend and drag it at least a hundred yards past the charge."

When they had finished, the tire ruts were marked as if something had come through not long ago, but nothing indicated that it had done anything more than pass through. "All right," Turenne said. "Places, my friends. Fighting should begin at the house in about twenty minutes."

At that moment they heard the distant growl of truck engines. Turenne gestured for them to hurry, and they ran for their places. Dan had farthest to go, and his exhaustion was beginning to catch up with him, but he locked in on getting the job done, focused on getting up to the rock he had picked.

As he settled in and began sighting his rifle where the first truck was due to appear, he relaxed and let himself ease into the job. If this phase went right, it would be frightening—they were downright crazy to do such a risky job—but it would not take long, and what needed to get done would get done.

The first truck crossed his sights. He sat perfectly still and watched the next one come, and the one after... each time tracking the driver until the truck behind appeared. As each truck appeared, it was a reprieve—probably only of seconds—for the driver of the one in front of it. Each fresh head that arrived removed Dan's interest in blowing apart the one ahead of it.

When the corner of his eye perceived the sudden burst of flame and smoke, he sighted in on the driver of the sixth truck. He was taking a careful lead already. All he

had to do was gently squeeze the trigger and take another shot before there was time for the first one to arrive. He squeezed again, and then, to be sure, fired four
quick shots at the back of the truck in hopes that
something back there would blow. As he fired the last
shot, he saw the driver slump forward, and the truck
surged to overtake and rear-end the truck in front of it,
slewing it around and forming a perfect roadblock.

Time began to pick up speed again. He heard the
crackle of flames in the wrecked trucks below, the gut-
tural shouts of orders, the chugging of an engine that
was not quite extinct yet.

He scanned forward to the front of the convoy and
saw disaster. Sutherland had been right: the charge had
all reflected upward. But the good that had done, tearing apart the lead truck, had been undone by one little
bit of overkill. The lead truck had actually flipped over
and rolled down into the ravine, leaving the road clear.
Even now the second truck was accelerating over the
crater, its tires and suspension bouncing crazily, running with everything he had to get out of there. The cab
was already past the point where he had any clear shot
at the driver. Dan wasted his two remaining shots, plus
a full clip, trying for the tires. He got at least three, he
thought, but unfortunately the driver was smart enough
to keep moving. Four shots into the next clip, the lead
truck rounded the bend. He turned his attention to the
bullet-riddled third truck, already out of Turenne's

range and rapidly escaping from Quentin's bursts from the BAR.

He didn't see the mortar round land, but the cab of the truck suddenly exploded, and it veered off to the side. Sutherland had gotten a lucky shot, but they were good however you got them.

As it tumbled down the canyon, the third truck exploded with a blinding yellow-white fury. Flames washed all the way back across the road and licked at the mountain itself. Whatever was in the fourth truck, whether it wasn't flammable or the driver was just lucky, he gunned his engine and got a long head start while everyone shooting was still blinded and shaken. He was around the bend before anyone could hit him at all.

The two trucks wedged against each other by the collision, the rear one with its driver dead, were now the only targets remaining, and Turenne and Quentin sprayed both, as if in fury for the ones that had escaped. Sutherland's mortar rounds dropped in the immediate area. The fourth one connected, setting the two trucks on fire and rupturing the cover on one of them.

At that moment thirty German soldiers came pouring around the bend from the remaining trucks in the convoy. Dan nailed the officer, a clean head shot with blood, hair and brains spilling out behind the running officer, and all of them fired into the press, but they had made no plans for a force of this size, and soon the Germans were joined by many more.

Dan saw Quentin get taken by a potato masher. The BAR had fallen silent, so perhaps he had run out of ammunition or maybe it had jammed. Turenne fired at the enemy soldier, and he fell, but the little black object sailed out of his hand and through the air, tumbling as it went. A low boom, a barely felt shock through Dan's stomach where he lay on the rock, and Quentin flopped halfway into view, his head hanging at a crazy angle. His body jumped twice as the Germans shot him to make sure.

Dan was sniping at everything he could find, but there were so many that he was unable even to make them stay under cover. They just kept scooting, dodging and zigzagging. In another moment they had overrun Turenne, and he was raising his hands in surrender. Sutherland was down, probably wounded rather than dead, but another prisoner for sure.

Samson sat back, looking at the bloody rising of the sun, promising a storm by day's end. He realized that none of the enemy was headed toward him. A quick scan of the hill showed no one advancing toward his position. They were all occupied with getting Sutherland onto a stretcher.

Turenne was being handcuffed and searched. This time they were more thorough, and Dan was a little amused at the sheer quantity of hardware they kept finding.

Meanwhile, a crew was busy toppling over the first of the two trucks blocking the road, apparently having determined that it could not move under its own power. From the careless way they handled it, it probably had contained nothing. The truck that Dan had scored on first was next. They unloaded a bunch of crates that were pretty clearly ammunition of some kind, and had Turenne take a seat on them.

Then they dragged out the driver and another body from the back of the truck. The two broken corpses did not make Dan feel any better. A mission that accomplishes nothing but murder is not a success. Every Vietnam vet knew you could come out way ahead on the body count and still not have accomplished a thing— except that somewhere, someone you didn't know was now widowed, orphaned, left without a hope in the world.

The two bodies were carried back into one of the trucks behind. Then they moved Sutherland, carefully, and at last Turenne.

Meanwhile, several soldiers were dumping rocks into the hole the charge had left. Another soldier fiddled under the hood of the crashed truck. Suddenly he stood up and made the circled thumb-and-finger, three-fingers up "okay" gesture—must have seen too many American movies, Dan thought sourly. They started the truck and sent it rolling down the hill to crash and explode in the ravine.

With the crater filled, there was nothing left for them to do but pull out. They clambered aboard the vehicles, and the convoy rolled on. The ambush had delayed them less than fifteen minutes. Dan didn't like to admit it, but he felt a certain sneaking admiration for the convoy commander. That was a damned fine job of getting going again in hostile territory, and he'd certainly handled the firefight like a pro.

He wondered what a good, professional soldier was going to think of Cabrini's crazy scheme. Maybe nothing. Professional competence didn't necessarily make a man moral.

With the convoy gone, and no rearguard left, Samson was free to come out of hiding. The sun was higher now, the last morning dark out of the sky, and it was promising to be clear and cold all day. Right about now the attack must be beginning at Cabrini's house. Flenstein would doubtless try to block the convoy, but he didn't really have enough men to deal with that and keep the house surrounded, so they would almost certainly get through. Maybe he'd get lucky and score some hits on the fuel trucks, but they couldn't count on that, either.

By the time Dan rejoined the platoon, it would probably all be over except the B-17 raid. The bombers would almost certainly get here before the weather closed in and would turn Cabrini's base into rubble, especially if the convoy arrived with enough rocket fuel. He might get there just in time for the fireworks, if he simply walked.

God, he was tired. His hands were in shreds from his escape the night before, he'd had no sleep or food since, and he was still bruised from all the stumbling in the dark and the beating Turenne had given him when he first arrived.

Too bad about Turenne getting caught like that. For an officer he was really a pretty okay guy. Well, he'd get some extra sleep, anyway, in a POW camp. . . .

If he ever got there.

Daniel Samson's brain was sleep fogged, but it wasn't totally without function yet.

The convoy, carrying Turenne and Sutherland, was going to Cabrini's house.

And so were the B-17s.

He needed to get there before the fireworks started.

Forgetting his tiredness, grateful to be able to move in daylight at least, Dan slung up his carbine and grenades and set off for Cabrini's at a dead run.

He realized that technically he should report back to his unit, but Flenstein would not be able to do anything unless he could penetrate the house, and if he could have done that they would not have needed the bombers. The only chance that Turenne and Sutherland had of getting out alive was one guy sneaking in and springing them.

Jackson Houston was going to take a little unscheduled leave so that Dan Samson could take care of unfinished business. The air was icy and clear, and the morning sun blindingly bright as he picked up a faster pace and held it.

The lieutenant had been pretty clever about it; Dan had to give him that. He had deployed a line that allowed all the automatic weapons to support each other, with two mortars to attack the house and two to cover the road. His position, scattered along a spur that pointed straight toward the house, would have been impossible to flank under cover in less than six hours. And not incidentally, since the "precision" bombing of World War II still meant that misses could be measured in miles, he had everyone spread out and thoroughly under cover, so that a missed bomb load would not take out the platoon.

It was working, too. They had probably tied down four times their number of Germans, sniping back and making sure they didn't rush the house, and the stray mortar rounds that dropped into the courtyard made anyone who was considering taking fully fueled rockets out pause and reconsider.

He was watching from a low hollow on the other side, seeing it from the German side. He stood low and scooted to the next hollow. He had worked out a route to the house from up above and had no more than five more dashes to reach the house.

He wasn't looking forward to that. Once at the house, he would have to admit that he didn't have the foggiest notion of what to do next.

He rose and dashed to the next hollow and, taking advantage of a spate of heavier fire, the one after that. There was an ominous silence, which might only mean that Flenstein was shifting some men under cover, but it could just as well signal a much bigger change.

While it sorted itself out, he would lie motionless and just breathe. He was very tired but couldn't afford to go to sleep.

How long had he been on the go? Less than forty-eight hours since he had come back to 1944, but back home he'd put in most of a full day first....

To take his mind off the hot, bunched feeling over his heart and focus his attention so that he would not simply drift off, he tried to figure out how long exactly it had been since he'd left his own time. He breathed deep and slow, trying to slow his heart rate, consciously relaxing and flexing his muscles to help get the lactic acid out of them. Of course, he knew what day it had been back home, and even that the crazy kid must have burst in with the AK at about 3:25 in the afternoon—now, what did Jackson Houston's memory say? This was February 14, 1944, Valentine's Day—and Dan Samson's birthday.

His lips stretched into a smile. It was too crazed, but it was true. Not only was it his birthday—it was the day of his birth. Somewhere over on the other side of the

Atlantic, Mom was about to give birth to little Danny. He wasn't sure what the time-zone difference amounted to, but he figured it hadn't quite happened yet, but was getting close now—for sure not more than three hours. She must already be at the hospital. They'd be phoning Dad at his squadron in Honolulu soon.

Gee, and nobody here had sent him a card or anything.

Maybe when he burst into Cabrini's house, they'd all jump out from behind the furniture and yell "Surprise!"

That almost made him laugh, which was a good measure of his tiredness. Sporadic sniping had resumed again, so he chanced a look, saw that things seemed as before and sprinted to his next hiding place, then to the next one. Now he was within reach of the French windows on this side.

As he jumped to his feet, he knew he'd been seen, though he could not have said what alerted him. All the same, he ducked and rolled, zigzagged—and heard the whining shot. He didn't know whether they had been close, but at least they had missed. He ducked, dived again, broke in another direction.

Two more shots.

Upper floor, he guessed, probably the third. He dived, rolled, heard something whine and hit the ground near him, was up and running once more. One sniper, so the alarm was not up for him everywhere in the house yet.

A bullet hummed by, and he instinctively veered. Less than twenty yards to go, and as the angle of depression got worse and more corners of the building began to interfere, this guy would have less chance of getting him.

He needed a diversion. First grenade, rip the pin out—too bad you really had to use both hands, and right now he wished the one-handed trick using your teeth would work the way it did in the movies. Pop it and throw! Like a long throw in from center to home, like a high, arching pilum hurled to land in the middle of a phalanx. It sailed up and over the housetop before clattering down the roof and blowing up in the inner courtyard. That ought to draw some attention.

Second grenade, another rip—that left three—and he threw a hard straight shot—just like pitching, just like using the sling in the pass at Mekh'hido.

He used the butt of the carbine to shatter the cheap little lock, and he came through the French doors into what looked like an unusually tasteless waiting room for an old-style brothel. There was more frill, lace and trim, all in white, than he had ever seen before in his life. Lacy curtains hung from intricate ironwork, white chairs were supported on legs that coiled like snakes, and two sofas stood on spindly twisted legs, covered by lumpy white spreads hung with tassels.

In the dead silence that lasted for a moment, he looked around the room, bemused, wondering how such a thing could ever have come to be. As he looked at it more, he realized it was clearly a terrible mistake, and with a mental bow to Turenne, he stepped through the door, unpinning a grenade and tossing it back into the room as he proceeded up the hallway. It was probably a waste of a grenade he would need later, but he was afraid the B-17s might somehow miss that room.

He hurried down the hall, hoping to find some clues about where Turenne and Sutherland were held. He would have to get to the other wing of the house, where the fighting was going on, if he was to get down to the secret chambers below the building, so he hoped they were being held back here, as far out of the line of fire as possible.

As he ran, he kicked doors open. Most of the rooms seemed to be empty except for very old furniture. The eighth door he kicked, a German stuck his head out. Dan gave him the butt in the teeth and stepped into the room, carbine leveled.

The first thing he noticed was that the arm he stepped over had a white armband with a red cross on it. Oh, hell, he'd bashed some poor harmless medic. The next thing he saw was a white sheet covering the top of a desk, with something beneath it—the size told him what he would find, but he flipped back the sheet to make sure and to get the dog tags if possible, since it would be a lot easier for Sutherland's family if he were KIA than MIA.

He looked. It took a moment for it to register. Then he turned and vomited onto the floor.

It was Sutherland, but his face was constricted in a ghastly grin, and in addition to the shattered knee that had disabled him, both his shoulders were dislocated and a bone had erupted through the muscles of his forearm. The eyes were wide and staring, but nothing short of a pair of pliers and a sail-maker's needle could have closed them.

Dan took the dog tags, then flipped the sheet back over.

Now he knew where Turenne was, but it might already be too late.

With the ruckus he had been making, for certain they knew he was in this wing, and they would be coming soon. But since he needed to get to the other wing, he decided to take a chance on the very last route they would have expected—straight across the courtyard.

As he started his sprint, something exploded behind him, probably a mortar shell. But he made the dash just fine, stepping through a courtyard window into what was plainly an office of some kind. On general principles, he opened the drawers of a file cabinet, tipped it over, broke a kerosene lantern over it and touched it off with his Zippo, before bursting through the door.

The hallway leading to the study was jammed with German soldiers, running, crouching, shouting orders. He tossed grenades each way, dived into the room across the hall and came up firing as the grenades exploded.

There were three windows, a German kneeling at each one, and it was just like a snap firing drill. He pulled the trigger three times, and the three soldiers fell away from the window, leaving the windowsills awash with blood.

Samson pivoted, returned to the hall and used the five shots remaining in the clip to make everyone in the hall duck for cover. Then he ejected the clip and slapped in the new one as he ran, and burst through the door of the burned-out study and on down into the wine cellars.

He landed in the middle of another battle. Gunfire rattled everywhere. His first thought was that the floor was running ankle-deep in blood, and then he realized that it was wine. He ducked low and tried to figure out what had happened. Was Turenne loose and taking them all on? Had Flenstein's men somehow gotten down here?

Something hard and round poked him in the back. "Drop your weapon, please."

He relaxed, planning his pivot and strike for a pistol disarm, knowing it could get him killed.

"You are Jackson Houston?" a crisp, Oxford-accented voice said.

"Yeah."

"Colonel Turenne said he thought you would turn up. I'm afraid we didn't believe him. Cabrini and his men are in the secret facility. It's all right—you can look around now."

He did, and found himself face-to-face with a German infantry captain.

"You see, Private Houston," the man explained, covering Dan with his pistol, "we were told only that this was a secret base and that the special supplies we carried were for a secret weapons project. I don't suppose there would have been any problem for Major General Schvantz—yes, that is Cabrini's real name—if he had simply accepted the supplies and gotten on with his business. But he had to show off. He had to show us what he wanted to unleash on the world, this damned sarin of his."

There was a burst of heavy firing, and the captain squatted down. Dan's concentration moved from how he could take the pistol away to whether he ought to. "So you saw what they did to Sutherland. Inhuman, isn't it? Bad enough to gag even a Nazi?"

"I would not know," the captain said. "I am not a Nazi. You might be surprised to know how many of us are sympathetic to the Anglo-American countries, how many of us secretly oppose Hitler. His crimes have dishonored the Reich and the Wehrmacht—his mistakes will bring ruin on us. Surely there is no real conflict between men of good will, be they good Germans or good Americans."

Yeah, right, Samson thought. All these good Germans just happen to be occupying Europe, but they're not really Nazis. Just accidentally they're keeping Eisenhower and Zhukov from liberating the death camps, but they don't really like Hitler. Heck, if they were just winning the war, they'd be standing right up for liberty right now, but in the present crisis . . . yeah, right.

He wasn't falling for this one. He'd heard too many political generals, ARVN and American, claim that this civilian leader or that political group tied their hands and forced them to keep losing lives. Too many captains and majors who thought the assassination program was "dirty" but were perfectly willing to carry it out.

He seemed to hear Master Xi chuckle in his head. *You see, wherever there is much danger, there is wisdom to be had. You have learned that when a man says "I have no choice," he is doing what he wants to.*

If the captain had simply said that the way Sutherland died had disgusted or horrified him, Dan would have bought it. A speech on principles was out of place, too cold for someone capable of mutiny motivated by horror, too calculated to be convincing and not enough honest expression of the guts.

The words came to Daniel Samson. Too prepared.

"Where's Colonel Turenne?" he asked.

"We simply did not believe what he tried to tell us. And so when we arrived and were conducted down to that chamber of horrors...well, it was not until we saw Sutherland and the colonel die that we knew what barbarity was prepared for the world."

Nice try, pal, Dan thought. If you'd known I came in the back way, I bet you would have had an even better story.

"And then—well, I ask you, sir—what else could we have done?"

"I understand," Dan said, keeping the disbelief from his voice. "And Cabrini, or whatever his name is, is still holding out down there."

"Yes."

"In the secret part of the house, behind the wine cellar."

"Yes." The captain was beginning to look impatient.

Samson was going to need a new way to stall, and soon. "So where is the problem? This place will be bombed level in an hour at most. He can't fuel up and launch by then. All you have to do is surrender to the Allied forces outside..."

"Surrender?" The shock slurred and deepened the Germans' carefully Oxfordized voice, so that it came out like an immigrant washerwoman on the East Side. "I have far superior forces in a superior defensive position! Don't be absurd!"

"Well, of course, since you put it that way..." Dan paused, frantically trying to think of an approach that would work. "How about an armistice or a truce? Time out to get Cabrini, and then..."

"I told you, I have a superior position." The captain's irritation was obviously rising by the moment. He began to explain slowly, as if to a very annoying small child. "It is not only a basic rule of warfare, it is the di-

rect orders issued by General Kesselring *himself*, that we
are not to—''

The gunfire was continuing, off and on as soldiers
dashed from cover to cover, followed by hot slugs, but
neither side was laying a glove on the other. So who was
fighting down here, and was there a side he would want
to be on?

The captain was finishing now, emphatically, ''So
you see that simply cannot be a solution acceptable to
me as an officer of the Reich.''

He looked over the captain's left shoulder. He let his
eyes get wide and his body startled. ''There's Cabrini
now!''

The captain involuntarily turned his head a fraction.
Dan whipped a low, knuckle-breaking kick to knock the
pistol aside, stepped in to draw the captain's arm forward by the wrist and thus put the pistol back behind
himself, reaped the captain's leg and landed a hard blow
with the heel of his hand on the captain's jaw. The captain's head whipped back, his feet rose eight inches off
the floor, and he descended in a beautiful backward arc
as Samson drove him downward until the crown of his
head smashed onto a bulge in the limestone floor, concealed by the two inches of wine sloshing around on
everything. The captain's skull broke with an audible
crack, and wine splashed upward to his waist even before Samson let him fall into it.

He grabbed for his carbine and breathed easier when
he saw it was apparently only damp and sticky with

wine on the outside. It had fallen onto a piece of broken old pallet, and the muzzle and firing mechanism had not gone under. He was sure going to catch hell at inspections for a while, though.

Not knowing what else to do, he simply shouted, "Hey, Colonel! Where are you and what side am I on!"

There was a wild, happy crow of laughter from far up toward where the passage to the secret chambers was, and an immediate lively exchange of gunfire. When that quieted, he heard Turenne's answering shout. "You can hear where I am. And as for what side, I believe you are on mine."

Samson could hear whispering and cursing, all in German, among the barrels. A helmeted head popped up, saw him, stared in horror and started to shout before the carbine barked and he fell, one of his eyes suddenly punched all the way through his head.

Immediately Dan crouched behind a barrel by a pillar and waited. One short moment later another helmet rose briefly above one of the racks, and Dan put a shot through it.

"How many snakes under this rock, Colonel Turenne?" he shouted just before he rolled over to the next pillar. A moment later bullets pinged off the pillar where he had been. By the muzzle-flashes in the dim basement, at least three Germans were in that corner over there, far enough back from Turenne. He pulled out one of his two remaining grenades, yanked the pin and hurled it. Turenne shouted something just before the grenade went off.

It had been a long time since Dan had been in an enclosed space, underground at that, with a grenade going off—not since the VC tunnels around Pleiku. He'd forgotten the way the blast pounded at you, the terrifying, mind-erasing jolt that shut everything down for a long second while everyone on both sides checked to see if he was still alive and unhurt and to see who wasn't.

Into that long silence floated Turenne's lazy, warm drawl, as if the whole war were over and he was pointing out some attractive young woman from a sunny sidewalk café. "Well, my friend, now that it is quiet enough to talk, I would say we had about a dozen opponents, but right now it's very hard to tell."

A shot reverberated in the basement. Samson saw the light of the muzzle-flash reflect off a wall, and pulled the trigger twice, hoping that the ricochet might do some good. There was some splashing around, probably just the guy moving to better cover, rather than any evidence that Samson had actually hit anything.

Turenne fired, then, three clear shots booming from the narrow passage, and there was a shallow splash.

"You okay, Colonel?"

"Quite. The fellow I was disputing with, though, is facedown in a third-rate red. I think there are only three or four of our enemy left, *mon ami*. Are you under good cover?"

"Fair." He was beginning to notice just how uncomfortable it was to lie on a frigid stone floor in two inches of wine, and he really hoped Turenne would come up with a plan to get him out of it soon.

There was another loud roar, and the wave of concussion beat into him. As his ears came back into the range of function, the first thing he heard was the trickling of wine from dozens of holes in fresh barrels.

Then screaming started. Somewhere out there, probably off to his right, a German soldier was hurt badly. The sound was a shriek, one that rose up till you could hear the last wisp of air rasp out through the wounded man's vocal cords, and then a sucking, a low gasp as he struggled to draw air back into his lungs.

In the vast cellar, with gaping barrels and angular walls, every shot and explosion had been followed by a long loud rumble that faded down into a tuneless ringing. But this was far worse. The groans, gasps and shrieks from that one badly wounded man echoed and reechoed for so long that they piled on top of one another. His voice became a whole miserable chorus of the damned, each gasp, sob and shriek a thousand souls burning forever.

Two grenades and many stray shots had taken a toll of the light bulbs that hung from the crude wooden grid ten feet up, so that now just four of them lit the vast cellar. Dan wondered why no one had turned the lights off, and then realized that neither side could have wanted to be down here in the dark.

The bare bulbs cast deep black shadows off the un-even stone, and between the eerie light, the lake of red on the floor and the never-ending screams, the cellar was a vision of hell in which no one wanted to move or act.

After a minute, and with no firing from either side, Turenne said in English, "Hold fire, Houston. I'm going to offer them a truce to get him out of here."

"We vill accept," said a voice to Dan's right and about twenty feet in front of him.

Turenne spoke rapidly in German, and an exchange followed. It seemed to take little time to settle the issues, then Turenne spoke to Dan in English again.

"All right, Private, they are going to stand up slowly, with hands raised, and we will hold fire. Their comrade is wounded in the abdomen, and it may take some time and effort to move him. They have agreed to leave the cellar to us, and you can search it as soon as they reach the stair landing. After you have confirmed that they have not left anyone living behind, you will signal that they may proceed upstairs. Once they have gotten through the door and the door is closed, the truce is over."

"Got it," Dan said.

Again Turenne said something in German, then called out to Dan, "They are beginning now."

Three sets of hands crept slowly above the barrels, then three helmets. The screaming of the wounded soldier did not stop. As they cautiously stood up, Dan saw that two had rifles, and one a submachine gun, on slings across their backs, where they would be difficult to reach.

Their faces gray with fear, now that they were exposed, they walked very slowly over to the wounded man. One of them swore when he saw his wounded comrade. Then they all bent and gently lifted the man, their heads rising slowly above the barrels again.

As they lifted, he screamed again, worse than all the times before, and apparently fainted. Then the cellar was quiet except for his rasping, slurping breath. It took them a long, slow, careful time to move between the barrels, working their way up to the stairs. As they came to the spot that allowed them to see Dan, he stood slowly, still keeping his rifle leveled and staying alert in case someone popped up firing.

Nothing happened.

They worked their way around the barrels. The soldier they were carrying had lost his helmet, or perhaps they had removed it. The hair that was not matted with blood was carroty red. His features, now hanging slack, were fine boned, with a spray of freckles thicker than Sutherland's had been.

From his chest to his knees his body seemed to be a mass of blood. There was at least one large wound in the abdomen, and flesh hung in a loose flap over the front of his coat near it. The grenade must have rolled right up beside him when it had gone off. There were half a dozen smaller wounds, as well, and Dan suspected one might be a sucking chest wound.

In Nam, Dan would have said the guy had around a one-third chance, but that would be with prompt helicopter evacuation to a good hospital. Most likely he would die and take hours to do it.

The three soldiers, two at his shoulders, one at his feet, carried him past without looking at Daniel Samson. He understood. What could anyone have said?

When they reached the landing, they stopped, and Dan began the quick, grim job of searching through the aisles between the barrels, moving as noiselessly as he could in the sloshing wine and listening for movement. He found six bodies and checked to make sure that all of them were dead. No question about the three that were shot through the head, but others had died of multiple wounds, mixing their dark, thick blood with the pale, thin wine, and these he had to search for a pulse or for a clearly fatal wound, there in the vast shadowy space with half the lights gone, loomed over by the great casks on all sides. Everywhere he could still hear wine trickling out of the barrels and tinkling into the pool through which he waded.

He went as quickly as he could, knowing a man was dying on the landing, knowing that ten minutes ago he had been trying to kill him and that in five more he might again be trying to kill his friends.

At last he was satisfied. "Colonel Turenne, it's all clear. No one left alive down here." He motioned to the men on the landing.

As they turned to head up to the door, Turenne called something to them. One of them turned just slightly and nodded, almost a solemn little bow to the French colonel, and although they could not move much faster with the badly wounded man, their pace seemed to have picked up a little.

"What did you tell them?" Dan asked.

"I have been debating whether I should tell them that in less than half an hour this place will be bombed into rubble. It finally got to be too much for me to imagine them carrying that man upstairs for a medic and then having him killed by the bombs. You get attached to the lives you spare, you know."

"Can I move back toward you?"

"Do it slowly. Make sure you keep the door covered. I have something that will interest you. I am coming forward, as well."

In a few seconds they stood beside each other, and prodded there at gunpoint by Turenne, Cabrini stood in front of them. Turenne had a German rifle, and his pockets were so filled with ammunition that he was probably a major explosion hazard himself.

"Good to see you, Colonel."

"I'm rather delighted to be here. Now, with good luck, those soldiers believed me and will be evacuating upstairs shortly. Then we simply walk our friend out the back of the building, very slowly and carefully, and re-join our forces. On the other hand, if they didn't believe me, they can direct a large force down here immediately. At least from here we can keep the door covered and delay them further. And, truly, if I must sit out an air raid in the midst of a stockpile of deadly gas, I would rather do it down here underground anyway."

Samson nodded agreement. "We can hope they'll see it our way. How the hell did you get loose and get our favorite Nazi villain as a hostage, anyway?"

"It would be an hour in the telling. It's enough to say that I did it the way Napoleon advised—I got a little bit of luck and made a great deal more of my own to add to it."

"Those idiots had not bound him," Cabrini said bitterly, "and then he created a diversion.... It was a crude, stupid trick, even if it worked."

"But it did work," Turenne added.

The door swung open, and Dan fired.

Half a dozen grenades, big, deadly potato mashers, flew in through the door and splashed into the wine. As one man, Turenne, Dan and Cabrini dived into the sloppy mess at their feet.

Nothing had flown back far enough to be near them, but the heavy booms of the grenades, designed as concussion weapons, brought blood from ears and noses, and some of the pillars broke. The ceiling above groaned audibly as masonry began to tumble from it.

"Back to the gas rooms!" Turenne shouted. Chunks of stone were booming off the hollow casks as Dan grabbed Cabrini's belt, yanked him upright and dragged him back into the corridor.

"At least we won't have to defend that room, if all that keeps falling," Dan said.

"We can hope. Damn, I wish I could be sure of getting a grenade rolled under the stairs—it would help if we could bring the stairs down."

Cabrini laughed. "So we all join together in the grave here."

Turenne turned at him and smiled, a strange, cold smile. "While we live, there is hope. While you are possibly valuable as a hostage, you live. Right now the possibility seems quite remote, but not zero. Would you care to avoid my becoming too emotional to estimate probabilities properly? Just at the moment, like most of us Mediterranean not-quite-supermen, I am feeling my racial tendency to be high-strung."

Cabrini glared at him, but he shut up.

Outside, the falling of stone seemed to have petered out into a spattering of gravel. "I better see what's up," Dan said, and crawled forward through the wine. He should have gotten used to the stuff by now, but if anything it was worse than the first time he had bellied down into it. He sure hoped that one of the very few spare sets of clothing being carried in the mule train would fit him, because by now these were surely permanently purple.

As he peered around the corner, he saw things he liked and things he didn't. The several fallen piles of rock would be perfect cover for the ten or fifteen German soldiers now descending the stretch of the stairs he could see. On the other hand, the last nine feet of stairs seemed to be gone, and the stairs were too slick and wet for men to lower themselves easily, so they were trying to find some way down.

Clearly they either didn't know about the back room or thought that Turenne and Samson were dead.

He announced his return to the living by shooting an officer in the head.

There was an immediate flurry of activity on the broken stairway. Some jumped off, taking their chances on dropping onto wine-slippery limestone, and Dan heard swearing and yelps of pain. One tried to run upstairs, and Dan let him go. Others milled around for a fatal moment of indecision, sensing how exposed their position was but unwilling to chance the leap.

If he'd had his old M-16, or even that heavy BAR, he might have wiped most of them out with one good hosing of full-auto, but since all he had was semiauto, he quickly lined up his targets, moving from one to the next, his finger squeezing the trigger in quick succession. He figured that of the five rounds he squeezed off before they had all jumped or fallen, at least three had found a target.

He grabbed for his last grenade, thinking to pitch it as they gathered to rush him.

A thought struck him, and as he pulled the pin, he threw it not at the enemy, but straight up into the broken and crumbled ceiling overhead. For the first time, luck was with him and there was a short fuse, or perhaps the grenade hung up on a shelf or ledge, because after it ricocheted off something up there, it blew while still close to the ceiling.

With a great booming, rocks began to drop again. Dan doubted he had brought down the ceiling yet, but at least they'd all be crouching under the stairs, waiting for the big stuff to stop falling, and with their officer dead it would probably take them a second or two to regroup.

He crawled slowly backward till he was out of line of sight from anywhere in the main room, then raced back down the passage. Turenne had gotten Cabrini most of the way to the steel door.

"They're slowed down, but not stopped," Samson reported.

"Best we could hope for. Let's get this door between us and them and take up a position somewhere, then see how it goes. How's your ammunition?"

"Six clips left. One or two rounds in the carbine. Call it about fifty rounds—not a lot if we have to last very long."

At the door, as they were trying to shove Cabrini through, he began to struggle again and landed a vicious kick on Dan's shin.

Then the bindings from Cabrini's wrists dropped to the ground, and tearing himself from their hands, he burst through the door and around the corner into the lab.

Samson pounded after him as Turenne shouted, "I shall hold them."

Putting his full trust in Turenne, Samson chased all thought of the enemy behind him out of his mind and concentrated on his pursuit of Cabrini. A door slammed as he came around the corner, not quite fast enough, so Dan saw which it was. His wet boots skidding on the linoleum, he raced to the door, tried the latch and found it locked inside.

The carbine bucked in his hand as he fired at the latch, but the round screamed off in a wild ricochet into the ceiling, and the steel was twisted but not broken. He yanked hard at the handle, and this time the handle came off in his hand.

Two more rounds finally broke the lock, and he cautiously kicked the door open.

There was a squeaky rumble, and he ducked and fired. Cabrini's voice, high-pitched with terror, swore at him in German, and then shrieked, "The gas is stored in here, you idiot!"

Samson looked up just in time to see a metal cart, its wheels squeaking, being pulled into the next room, and to see that his shot had bored a bole in the plaster precisely between two glass bottles, just inches apart, identical to the one he had seen used to kill the dog.

He dived for the cart, grabbing its legs, and found himself in an absurd tug-of-war with Cabrini on the other side. On the cart were several large metal canisters, and just above where Cabrini gripped the other legs and fought grimly to drag it into the chamber, where Senneman had died, was another glass bottle of sarin.

Behind Cabrini, he glimpsed at least a dozen other canisters of sarin, already moved into the observation room while he had been struggling with the door.

THE FIRST ONE brave enough to open the door was shot dead on the spot. Turenne was rather proud of such a clean, neat shot. The grenade that dropped through a moment later rolled about two feet. Turenne withdrew around the corner where he had staked out his position, waited for the explosion, flipped around the corner again and put a bullet through two of them as they came in. In response, the back wall was sprayed with a submachine gun.

He hoped that Houston had stalled or stopped Cabrini, because his best guess was that about the eighth man through the door would reach his corner, with about a fifty percent chance of getting past . . . and the tenth man would be stepping over Turenne's corpse shortly after.

The autofire stopped, and Turenne stood alongside the corner, drew a breath, held it, whipped up the German rifle and fired head high around the corner, first downward into the head of the soldier who was crouch-running along the short hallway, then into the face of the one behind him. For good measure, he fired two more shots through the doorway.

By now the place was getting so packed that he knew he had hit something. By his count, he had taken out six of the enemy, and as the bullets from the German sub-machine gun tore holes in the wall in front of him, he reloaded and thought, I may not even make number eight. And I would like to reach ten.

He chanced a pop shot along the floor and got the one with the submachine gun. That stopped them a split second, and he was able to fire another chest-high shot through the doorway, probably getting yet another.

Eight.

Well, those had been mere luck, so he would try for twelve.

Again bullets raked the back wall, and it occurred to him that they probably did not know what was stored in there if they were spraying ammunition around so freely. Well, if he must die, let it be in the process of educating a few Germans.

He glanced down and saw that, somewhere along the way, a bullet had taken off two fingers on his left hand.

He looked away from it. He didn't need those fingers at the moment anyway.

Another helmet popped out, and his trigger finger squeezed.

That made nine.

FLENSTEIN HAD had better days, but at least the basic mission was getting accomplished. With the sun well up, the enemy were still pinned down in the house, and at last mortar fire got a couple of fires going. That made the Germans inside more vulnerable as they were forced to extinguish the fires, and sometimes a sniper would get a clear shot. There was less enemy fire from the house now, either because they were low on ammunition or a lot of men were detailed to fight fires.

Beside him, Scott nodded with grim satisfaction. "Too bad our guys didn't stop that convoy, even if they caused some damage. But we're holding them, and the planes are due now."

As if on cue, there was a wonderful, faint roar in the air. Flenstein signaled the forward squad to try again now that the enemy fire had slackened. Kowalski, a big Polish kid who'd been an outfielder in minor league before getting drafted, managed to put phosphorus grenades, one right after the other, into three upper-floor windows. In ten seconds there were three more big fires going, and to Flenstein's great satisfaction, black smoke poured from the house. A low boom inside told him ammunition or rocket fuel had gone off, as well.

Four B-17s were wheeling around, ten miles out, to come in out of the sun, low over the ridge. Probably there would be no ground fire to avoid, but they did not know that.

1a1

Wartide

Flenstein signaled for one more set of phosphorus grenades from Kowalski, who obligingly bagged three more windows.

"You know, I used to see him play back home for the Heber Springs White Sox," Scott said, "and back then he couldn't have made a throw to home if the whole world depended on it."

The lieutenant grinned. "Some guys come through in the clutch. Okay, signal a pullback while there's still time—the flyboys aren't nearly as accurate as they think they are, even with a target that obvious."

Covered by heavy firing from behind, with only a scattering of answering shots from the house, the platoon began to retreat over the ridge. The drone of the B-17 engines filled the air again. Flenstein looked up into the sky to see that the house was now surmounted by a great column of inky black smoke. On a clear day like this, they must be able to see it all the way to Cassino. In a while there would be nothing left of the place.

"It's all over," he said.

"HEY, MAN, YOU CAN give it up and still sit out the war in a POW camp," Samson said to Cabrini as the cart wobbled between them. "No way are you going to launch your rockets." He knew he didn't sound right for the period, and he didn't care anymore. "Some of that booming upstairs is probably the fuel going off right now."

Cabrini glared and kept tugging. Then, as fast as a striking snake, he kicked out and crushed the fingers on one of Dan's hands. Dan's grip slipped, and the cart rumbled after Cabrini into the isolation room.

The German agent tried to slam the door, but Dan had thrown his body into the crack. It knocked the wind out of him, but he got through, dragging his carbine with him.

The counterweighted door swung closed behind him and locked with a cold clank. It was just the two of them. Dan's carbine was leveled on Cabrini, and high over his head, Cabrini held the glass bottle of sarin. "If you fire," he said, "I assure you we are both dead." He drew a grenade from his clothing. "You probably did not trouble yourself with the question 'Where does the gas go after they are done?'

"The answer is that anything can be diluted to harmlessness if the volume is only large enough. You may hear, if you listen, the sighing of air in conduits and the powerful fans that purge the air in this room.

"The air exhaust is about half a mile downwind of here, and occasionally we found a dead goat or rabbit somewhere near the exhaust. Even diluted by many cubic meters of air, it is powerful enough to kill at very close ranges.

"Now I don't know which way the wind is blowing at the moment. I don't know, because I've had no time to compute what the dilution would be if we put the four and a half tons of sarin that are stockpiled in here through the pipe. Perhaps not enough to do anything, or perhaps it won't blow in the right direction.

"But perhaps it will be enough to call attention to the weapon. Maybe that helps your allies and warns them, but maybe it gets the führer's attention. I have prepared a few notes on the subject, and maybe our Intelligence will be sent to find out what is happening. Who can say? It may help us, or you... but from my viewpoint the war is lost if something doesn't happen. What is this called in your American football—a punt, I believe? Just kicking the ball down the field to see what happens?"

He smiled. Dan suddenly felt that nowhere in the faces of the hundreds of damaged souls that had passed through the homeless shelters Sarah had run had he seen such madness. He had helped with an investigation of an atrocity in Vietnam, testified against a chaplain who had raped and killed three little girls, and that chaplain, despite the glint in his eye, had been as cold, calm and sober as any bank president, compared to the lunacy that shone out of Cabrini's eyes.

A thought flashed into Dan's mind. I have seen it before... but not in these two lives. The answer must lie somewhere else in the Wind Between Time.

And Daniel Samson began to see what was going to happen, and why it had to. Fear settled down into his stomach like a gigantic ball of cast iron, cold as the freezing winter nights in the Italian mountains.

Because he saw what his role had to be, and nothing—nothing since he had first looked out through Jackson Houston's eyes scant days ago—was more frightening than what he must do.

Anything...anything but that, he thought at the back of his mind, hoping Master Xi or some other voice from the Wind Between Time would hear him and answer. Just name it, and I will do anything but that. You know I am not a coward. You must know that.

No answer came.

Cabrini continued to babble, wild chains of logic and speculation, a thousand crazy schemes about saving the Nazi dream that had claimed a quarter century of his life and that would bring it to an end in another few minutes.

If Daniel Samson could just find the nerve.

TURENNE WAS ALMOST HAPPY. For eleven generations, serving the ancien régime of the Bourbon kings and all the wild profusion of republics and empires that had followed it, the Turennes had fought for France as professional soldiers. Many of them had perished in battle, including Turenne's father in the trenches of the Argonne, and indeed, a part of Turenne had always thought the same fate might befall him, as well.

Another shot rang off the wall. Why had they not used more grenades? Perhaps they were out of them, or perhaps they did know something of the horrible death that sat crouched in cylinders down here, waiting only to be released.

Turenne was no longer bothering to shoot back on single shots. They were obviously intended only to annoy him. They had so far annoyed him out of two fingers on his left hand, and a stupidly painful flesh wound on the back of his head from a ricochet.

He was up to fourteen, and he thought that when the time came for him to be standing before the rest of the Turennes somewhere in the hereafter, he would have a good, solid score to claim…. Except, of course, that he had no children. He hoped they would understand that he had been quite busy and had simply not happened to father any. For that matter, there was also wine yet to be drunk, music yet to be heard, nights of theater and conversation and afternoons in the country.

He really wanted to live through this, little as he expected to.

Turenne had been pressing his jaw to the wall, using bone conduction to listen for footsteps. At that moment he heard the faint thudding of two sets of boots. Perhaps because he was so tired, and just wanted it over with, he rolled over into the hallway and blazed away with the rifle, hitting everything he could see, not caring if he died. He got the two onrushers in the face because they could not fire back accurately or quickly enough while running. As they fell, they uncovered two other men with rifles, standing at the bend of the hallway, and twice Turenne hastily aimed and squeezed the trigger.

To his astonishment—perhaps it had been his desperation, perhaps merely his luck, perhaps simply that God did not permit the Turenne line to end while France might yet need it—he had hit all four men squarely in the head. Four shots and four dead Boche. He scanned for the next one through his sights.

There was no one there.

The only opponents he faced were the misshapen gray bags lying there in the hallway, slowly leaking blood onto the floor.

He had won.

Gingerly he brought his feet under him and stood slowly up. The back of his head burned like fire, and the stumps of his missing fingers were bleeding steadily and aching.

He had won.

His spirits began to rise. Life was going to go on, assuming that Houston, good man that he was, had cornered or killed Cabrini.

And if he had not, some help might turn the balance.

He turned, put one foot in front of another, noticed that he was staggering like a drunkard and did not care. He headed down the hall, looking for Houston and Cabrini.

THEY HAD PULLED the last ones out and had formed a good, safe line near the top of the ridge by the time the B-17s finally made their run. To be accurate at such ranges, the planes had to come in low and slow, just hopping over the ridge and dumping their load onto the blazing house.

It was a great set of ringside seats. Lieutenant Flenstein and Sergeant Scott watched with satisfaction as the four B-17s, line astern, roared over the ridge. The first one dropped a bit short, and the third a little to the north of the house, both chewing up a lot of dirt for nothing, but the full bomb loads from the second and fourth planes crashed into the house.

After the first load to hit home, the building was plainly just a hollow shell, filled with fire. After the second, the walls collapsed or flew apart, and there was nothing left but a hot pile of rubble and a great scattering of embers, some of the embers as big as railroad ties.

"Sir? Here's the runner you sent to check on the ambush," Scott said.

One look at the runner's face, and all of the satisfaction from the air raid drained out of Lieutenant Flenstein. "What did you find?"

"Three destroyed trucks that I could see. Quentin was dead. I found the place where the other guys set up, but they weren't there."

From below came the grinding rubble of a basement caving in. The runner looked down and exclaimed, "Holy shit! Oh God! Uh, sorry, sir—"

"No, you're absolutely right. If you'd said anything else I wouldn't have thought you were human. Yes, chances are that they were taken down there as prisoners."

SAMSON STOOD THERE, stock-still, paralyzed with fear for the first time in many long years.

If he let Cabrini blow up those canisters, a great cloud of death would belch out of this room, through the exhaust ports, to float over the countryside. It might be entirely harmless, or it might not. It would kill Daniel Samson and Cabrini for certain, but it might take thousands more with it, and it might alter the whole course of the war, unleash worse horrors than the ones that had scarred Dan's own time.

But if he shot Cabrini, the glass bottle of sarin he held was almost certain to break—in fact, the effective thing might just be to shoot the bottle and not worry if the bullet then used Cabrini as a backstop. In that case, too, they would both be dead.

Yet there was one slim reed of hope, a hope only for Samson.

It did not sound as though Cabrini really wanted to die for a slight chance to alter history. He sounded frightened, terrified out of his mind, babbling with terror and trying to persuade himself that now, when the entire end point of all his schemes was reached, he was not going to funk it.

He was a man fighting fear and losing, and sooner or later some luck might break Dan's way while Cabrini dithered. Maybe Turenne would somehow fend off that whole attacking force, burst in and save the day, though Dan couldn't really imagine it. Maybe Turenne would just hold them off, but Flenstein and the platoon were even now bursting down the stairs, charging through to the rescue....

But a whole army could make no more difference, and make no more choices, than could Daniel Samson. They might lift the choice from him, but it would not get easier, and it would merely crush someone else instead, at best.

Why did it have to be something that produced such a terrible death? Why did it have to be the thing that he had seen shatter bone with its horrible muscle contractions, a thing that left you staring down the tunnel of eternity with a grin of deepest agony?

In his imagination he could feel his muscles pulling back, feel his jaw forcing him to bite through his tongue, feel his femurs erupting and his heart squeezing into a hard lump of pure pain. He imagined what it would be like, every horrible moment, and he could not face the thought.

This was what he had been brought here to face as Jackson Houston.

Despite Houston's secret, sneaking fascination with what other people thought of him, he would face this one alone, would die never knowing what they had made of the way his body was found. So that even the one thing that might have made it worthwhile to face the fear was never going to be granted to him in any form for which he had any use.

He had been given this chance to redeem his past incarnation because, after who knew how many incarnations, he had finished one as a brave and decent man. But was it worth it? How could it matter that the rest of those lives changed? The world had managed just fine with Jackson Houston as a lying, pimping sneak. It would make very little difference in the grand scheme whether he was a good, brave soldier or the lowest bastard in the Army.

Hell, the Germans had not used nerve gas. He knew that from history, anyway. So whatever he did, there was going to be no such effect as the one Cabrini was talking about. Cabrini was speculating, and there was even a certain frightening quality to his speculations, but he really did not know. Daniel Samson knew, and knowing that, he could be assured that it made no difference.

Jackson Houston could be a hero, or he could simply stand here and let Cabrini babble until something—Turenne, Flenstein, the other Germans, the B-17s, Cabrini's own disordered mind—took the whole matter right out of his hands.

And his being a hero would make no difference at all.

"You see," Cabrini was saying, "I need only set this grenade to explode, drop it among these canisters and count on the fan and the exhaust pipe to do the rest. Nearly five tons of sarin drifting downwind . . . surely something will change by my doing that. Surely when I have given my life to the Reich, the Reich will reward it by surviving, growing, conquering the world. There is point and beauty in falling as part of the conqueror's army, but there is nothing to be gained by becoming one more of those slain to round out the victory totals in the history books."

"The history books?" Dan asked to keep him talking. At least while he talked, he did not threaten to blow the canisters with the grenade.

"Yes, the history books. What other thing is there for us, except finally what we are known for and what others will think of us? And what is history except the judgment of all of humanity on which few men were truly important? And who is to write history except those descended from the victors of the past?"

Dan sighed. "What do you think of yourself, Cabrini? Really? I mean, okay, so you started out as a loyal German soldier and all that, but nowadays you just believe whatever the Nazi Party tells you to, and you spent all your time and effort coming up with a scheme so that sometime way in the future, a bunch of bored ten-year-old Nazis can try to remember your name? Is that so important you're willing to slaughter

God knows how many innocent people, and maybe your own side, just for a chance it could happen?''

Cabrini's eyes got a faraway look, and Dan could tell he was genuinely thinking about the question. At least the thinking made him quit toying with arming the grenade. That was a big advantage.

Of course, he knew what answer he'd give Cabrini if he'd just listen. You didn't face danger or treat people decently because of the way you would be remembered. You did it because that was the way you were, because you could feel the good in you and you weren't willing to lose it.

Suddenly he knew his own reason for pulling the trigger. Without hesitating, he lowered his M-1 to his hip, the position he'd learned to shoot well from in Vietnam.

He looked fear in the eye and knew he was bigger than it was and put everything out of his mind except hitting the target.

He squeezed . . . and watched the glass bottle fly into bits, saw the incredulous stare on Cabrini's face.

Maybe he should make this quick. He had been holding his breath to shoot. Now he drew in a great lungful.

It wasn't like he had imagined. It was worse.

TURENNE WAS ROOTED to the spot, not daring to speak and possibly distract Houston for a critical instant. The ravings of Cabrini made it clear that the worst could happen at any moment, and yet the man was clearly afraid, holding off taking the final step that would bring a horrible death on him.

Houston's answer to the ravings, it seemed to Turenne, was masterful. A simple question sent Cabrini's mind spinning, forcing him to think and relax his grip on the grenade.

He saw Houston's hand tense and the carbine take aim, and knew that it was the only way. A man does not lightly throw his life away, and when someone with Houston's judgment and courage did it, it was because he had seen something that left him no choice.

The sarin burst from the bottle like an evil genie in a story, the color and density of a puff of breath when the air is just cold enough to show it.

As Houston's muscle spasms set in, Turenne reached for his cap, but it wasn't there, so he moved his hand to the salute and stood at full attention as Houston and Cabrini, hero and devil, sank to the floor of the isolation chamber.

A second later, when the load of bombs brought down the roof, Turenne was still standing there. He had just enough time to feel himself pinned in the wreckage, to realize he had not been killed outright, when darkness fell upon his mind.

DAN'S HEAD FLEW BACK as his neck muscles contracted, and he felt everything tensing. The deep breath he had drawn screamed out through his overtight vocal cords, shredding them bloody, and then his chest was locked down and would not open up again. His back arching, he felt his features pulled into that horrible grin, felt his fingernails bite flesh and keep digging into his fists, broke his own thumb with the fingers of the same hand, and then came the other hand.

He felt the white-hot spear of pain as his scalp muscles tightened to terrible pressure all over his skull.

But despite his best effort to pass out, he was still conscious as the violent spasms broke his thighbones and drove them out of his flesh.

At last dark descended, after two seconds and all of eternity. He could feel the Wind Between Time beginning to howl. Behind him there was a rumbling crash that might have been an avalanche or the fall of the last ramparts of his brain.

Somewhere, faint, high, sweet and clear, a trumpet of triumph was playing in the Wind Between Time.

Back in the chamber, there was no one there to see as Samson's body simply vanished from under the pile of rubble that had covered it. With a groan and a rumble, the rubble settled, then more followed, including blocks of stone. In a moment the canisters rested safely under tons of wreckage, and above them a rough slope had opened to the sky.

A watery, blurred beam of sunlight stabbed through the midmorning cloud cover, reached into the hole and settled comfortably on the exposed back, shoulders and right arm of Colonel Turenne, and that was what drew the attention of Flenstein's platoon a few minutes later.

11

Daniel Samson blew and drifted through the Wind Between Time, and as he examined everything that had happened, his puzzlement only increased.

But I know the Germans never used nerve gas, he heard his own thought. *And Jackson Houston...*

He reached to find out, and discovered. In his own past, Jackson Houston had raped the girl after Bronski was done. When the German patrol came by, finding him in the act, he and Bronski had been taken prisoner. Flenstein's platoon had been attacked by surprise, and had lost the same men, in mostly the same ways, only three days earlier and a few miles to the southwest of where it had happened just now.

Something had well and truly died inside of Jackson Houston with that rape. Some last shred of anything decent, of anything with any promise.

The next day, not wanting to bother transporting prisoners who were already guilty of a capital offense, the same German captain he had faced in the basement had tried Bronski, using the evidence Jackson Houston gave in hopes of saving himself, and in about ten minutes had convicted him and "given him the noodle"— put a bullet to his head through the back of his neck, the execution reserved for partisans and spies.

Jackson Houston, trusting no one and moreover knowing full well that the captain was bound to find a reason to execute him as soon as possible, had gotten a very short distance. He had managed to overpower two guards while pretending to need to take a leak. To cover his own tracks, he thought, he had bashed in the captain's skull with a rock. But he had been shot dead as he stepped out of the captain's tent, by the man whose broken body Dan had seen taken upstairs in the shattered wine cellar.

Before the German patrol made it back to base, it was caught in the open by a flight of roving Mosquitos, British light bombers dispatched to harass targets of opportunity, and the scales of death had balanced again.

And Cabrini—what had originally happened to him?

Daniel Samson began to laugh soundlessly, there in the great dark of the Wind Between Time.

At the same instant that Private Jackson Houston had been stopping a bullet with his forehead, Cabrini, working late and alone preparatory to his launch, had stumbled and fallen facefirst onto a table where four of the deadly sealed bottles of sarin were stored.

Hearing the crash, one of his men had rushed down and opened the door, and the gas had spread through the house, killing as it went, finishing off men in their beds.

Before the arrival of central heat and natural gas, any large house in winter had always had several fires banked for the night. With no one to attend to them, they kept on smoldering. A gust of wind down a chimney put a spark on a carpet. The spark smoldered half-heartedly for a while, but at last the rug grudgingly began to burn. Then the sofa and the curtains erupted into flames, the fire raced through the house unfought, and the rocket fuel and oxidizer went up.

In the dead of night, the blazing torch of the house drew the attention of bombers like a light bulb attracting moths, and once again the sarin, cooked to harmlessness, was buried under tons of rubble.

So, Dan thought to himself. *What I did really didn't matter at all. Whether Jackson Houston was a rat or not, nothing was going to happen.*

But even as he thought it, he knew it was not true. For though there had not, as it turned out, been any need for the operation, something had happened to Jackson Houston. The part of his mind that would always be Jackson Houston was still rough and stained inside him, Samson noted, but it was now somehow clean at the core.

One small part of the burden of centuries had been lifted. All of the terrible battles of the past three days had been nothing more than the first step in a journey of millenia.

You have always fought for your country, Daniel Samson, whichever country it has happened to be.

And now you fight for yourself—not to defend yourself, for most of you is already lost—but to take yourself back from what you have been.

Dan thought he recognized the voice. It was Master Xi.

That is a face and a name I have worn, a way I have gone through the great circle and come out on the other side. Just as you have been Jackson Houston, I have been Master Xi. But all of us are much more than our names.

So everyone came here, sooner or later.

Some do. You do. That ought to be enough for you. That and your chance, now, after so many millenia lost, to find your way home.

Will I know anyone there?

It is the only place where you can really know anyone.

The answer made little sense, but Dan was growing tired. He would drift here—a little while was no time at all in the Wind Between Time—and then descend to begin another step. Then he heard somebody else call to him.

Houston, are you here? Where are we? The voice was Turenne's. Dan turned to find him, and somehow, with no sense that he could name, he perceived clearly Turenne, almost but not quite departing from his battered, brutally wounded body, and understood how much would be left undone if Turenne crossed over now.

I am here. You are going back. Just relax and let the clay draw you back into itself, he thought at Turenne.

I see something behind you—no, in you, Houston. I realize . . .

See me as I am, if you like, Dan thought.

In the way that the eyes of love, in seeing us, show us what we are, Daniel Samson felt Turenne really seeing him, saw the great dark stain of his past lives spreading through time, and the little patch he had gained by reconquering Jackson Houston. For one moment he saw, whole and complete, the battlefield that was everyone's soul and felt the horror and savagery of the struggle ahead, but also its glory and the value of the prize to be won, for what could be more valuable than the soul itself?

Then, tenderly, gently, he released Turenne's soul from his clasp, back into the circle of pain.

IT TOOK THEM FOREVER to get back down the hill with Turenne in the stretcher. Lieutenant Flenstein thought the whole way that he would die any minute, or surely during the frozen, stormy night that followed the day's scant miles, but if anything the Frenchman seemed to get a little stronger. Four days after they had been scheduled to make their rendezvous, the colonel hanging on to his life, rations and men exhausted, they reached Colli al Volturno, and loaded the still-unconscious colonel onto a truck headed for Naples. Then, after six hours of sitting around pointlessly, they were loaded into trucks themselves and sent down to rest camp in Naples.

There had not been many intact platoons within the Thirty-sixth Division after the failed attacks across the Rapido, and there was one fewer now.

While the division came back together, joined by new men, the veterans could recover, except for the lieutenant, who had to face massive paperwork and debriefing, even more of it after Turenne regained consciousness.

One late afternoon, basking in the warm sun, the scene so unlike the mountains that Naples might have been on another planet, they sat in the hospital ward with an officious, busy interviewer from Fifth Army, whose job apparently was to gather material for posthumous decorations.

"And you definitely saw Private Houston die?" the interviewer asked Turenne for the fiftieth time.

"*Oui.* Yes, I did. If it is that urgent, you can go up and dig for the body."

"We haven't, but OSS has, trying to find out about this new type of poison gas. They found Cabrini, and their man Senneman, and a lot of others, but no one who can be identified as Jackson Houston. And given the man's past record, and what you yourself have told us, Lieutenant, we have to consider the possibility that he somehow survived and used the opportunity to desert. We don't want to give him a Bronze Star posthumously, and then after the war have him turn up running a string of whorehouses in Palermo. Surely you see how bad that could look. General Clark has been very specific about making sure medals are earned."

"Any medal you give him, he will have earned," Turenne said. "And I am afraid he is quite, quite, dead. I saw him die, and I saw the rubble come down on his corpse. If they keep digging, the OSS will find it sooner or later, I'm sure."

"They've already stopped looking for the body," the clerk said. "There's higher priority stuff to do there, and the working conditions are terrible."

Lieutenant Flenstein cleared his throat and added, "Well, I knew Private Houston pretty well, I suppose...he was in my platoon for more than six months. I wrote a lot of that record, you know, and it really shouldn't figure too heavily in all this. He didn't desert, I can tell you that. That would not have been like him."

"No," Turenne agreed. "That would not have been like him at all."

The clerk from HQ looked from one to the other and saw that they would consider no other possibility. Well, the regulations said you had to go with the word of officers in the field, no matter how obvious it was that they were biased. He finished filling out the form and had them both sign it. When he went to hand the clipboard to the French colonel, he saw the two missing fingers on the left hand.

That was the trouble with war, the clerk thought as he drove away in the jeep that had been assigned to him. Some of the stuff you had to see! He'd need a good stiff drink before he went to bed tonight.

DANIEL SAMSON WAITED alone in the Wind Between Time for a long, long while. He used the time to probe, to ask, to understand, and finally he found that there was one question that he could not answer.

But why me?

Why did Daniel Samson have to be the one to clean up the mess? And why was there a mess in the first place? He could feel, stretching back into time, the immense weight of the crimes and evils committed by all his previous selves, of every act from petty cheating to foulest treason, and yet . . .

The answer he got was only that he could not yet bear the answer. That he had been doomed, doomed for millenia, to wander from life to life, with every possible predisposition to become, again and again, the worst possible soldier. And that he had fulfilled his doom so many times should have been no surprise.

There had been but one possible release. If, somehow, despite a rotten start and ample opportunity to go wrong, he had managed to resist, managed just once to make a good soldier and a good man of himself, he could win only this: the right to try to reclaim his past.

The right to try, nothing more.

Looking back now, he could see that Daniel Samson could have easily been like the rest. After the war, his father had deserted the family. They had been poor when he was growing up, but the good school district his mother had found them a home in had contained plenty of wealthy children who had spurned him and made fun of him, which ought to have lit the fires of envy and resentment, but somehow this time had not. His honesty had never been rewarded; rather, it had cost him things dear to his heart, over and over again, and his integrity had been punished at every step. He had loved girls who treated him like dirt, worked for crooked bastards who had cheated him, gotten bloody and bruised as a lineman so that rich-kid backs could look like heroes.

Yet, perhaps because of his mother, maybe just by luck, he had not become corrupt.

The dirty little war in Indochina—fought for goals that were fuzzy at best, judged by body counts as if the whole thing were a shopping expedition for cuts of meat, despised by many, hated by those who were there, systematically forgotten by the politicians until a decade later they dragged out the veterans for election-year parades—that had been a perfect opportunity to go bad. A thousand times he could have raped, looted, murdered for the hell of it, fragged officers he hated, gotten rich off heroin and dope.

Even after he got back, he could have blamed his problems on the war, laid enough guilt on Sarah to enslave her forever, traded on his war record to become a big-shot businessman or politician.

The range of what he could have done was endless, and yet he had not. For no reason he had understood at the time, he had clung to his personal integrity, held on and kept it, as if fighting for his very soul.

Maybe, on some level, he had known.

Because now, having done this, he had a chance. So far, in facing his pain and fear as Jackson Houston, he had taken one step down the long road. Future steps might be harder, and if life came with no guarantees that things would turn out, this afterlife came with even less.

It didn't matter. Now that he had truly thought it through, this was all he would have wanted anyway. Just a chance to make it all right.

Just a chance.

IT WAS LATE SPRING of 1963. Paris had never been so beautiful, Turenne thought, for in this spring there were no rumblings of danger from right or left, no risk of rebellion or civil war, and after the crises of recent years, far less danger, as well, that the Americans and Soviets would decide to settle matters across the bloody body of Europe.

He was early, and so he took his time on the way to the small, private military academy of which he was commandant, stopping to have his already mirror-bright shoes shined just for the pleasure of sitting in the little stand and looking out on the crowds in the busy street.

Yes, it was a good spring, and a time to reflect on the joys of being alive and on having done well at life. Not merely at the war, but, he had been pleased to note, when the dark threat of a civil war over Algeria had hung over France not so long ago, every one of the officers who had been boys at his academy had lined up for the republic. Making them officers was hard, but making them patriots was harder—and making them wise patriots, hardest of all.

He had never spoken to anyone of the vision he had seen, of how sometimes the smallest turnings can make a vast canyon of difference between the possible roads a life might take, but he thought perhaps that his life after the big war was really nothing but a carrying out of that vision.

His shoe-shine finished, he checked his watch. Good, plenty of time. He wandered up the street slowly, savoring the prosperity he saw, savoring the fact that no one here lived in fear, that even across the German border there was no lurking danger—well, not for some distance, anyway. Every new dress and fresh suit, every bunch of flowers and shiny new car, every newspaper that carried news and not propaganda, seemed to warm his heart.

At last he came to the cathedral, bought the candle at the little stand outside and went in.

His students thought he was very devout, he knew. In fact, he was not. He was not sure that he believed in any of this. But for the sake of things he could not quite name, as regularly as he brushed his teeth or paid his bills, Turenne came here to light a candle and to say a prayer for the soul of Daniel Samson.

THE WIND BETWEEN TIME howled dark and cold, and Dan at last felt ready to choose. He looked down over the great, tangled, messy line he had left in time, chose a moment without hesitation, and felt himself racing swiftly back, further and further into time, and then descending....

He opened his eyes on bright sunlight and began the next step of his long march back through eternity.

AFTERWARD

Americans have always had a problem with political wars, and even more with political wars that didn't work out well, and most of all with the veterans of those wars. Vietnam, of course, is the prominent and recent example.

But there have been other wars, and other campaigns, that were undertaken just as foolishly and forgotten just as callously. The history of the Italian front during the Second World War is painfully instructive in the dangers of a war waged by committee and compromise, where finally the purpose of the war becomes only to sacrifice more so that the previous losses will not have been for nothing. Those who thought we should never have gone down that road in the first place—people as diverse as Eisenhower and Stalin—could not win a consensus for stopping where we were, before more blood was shed over ground that, in their honest opinion, no longer mattered. Those who believed there was something to be gained there—Churchill, de Gaulle, Montgomery and Patton among them—could not win a consensus to give the American Fifth and the British Eighth armies anything like the resources they needed.

And so the whole weight of the half-made, half-hearted decision fell on the necks of the infantrymen who worked their way north, a rock and a hole at a time, in weather and terrain as bad, and against defenses as tough, as any in the war. Individually there was as much heroism there as anywhere, and as much endurance or wretched conditions. The men and the units who fought that thankless, forgotten campaign proved themselves as good as any in history.

But at the collective level, the campaign was being forgotten even as it was being waged. The celebrated 442nd Regimental Combat Team, made up of Americans of Japanese ancestry, was sent to Italy because no one else wanted them. Most of the few African-American combat units ended up there for the same reason. The day of the Normandy invasions, a member of Churchill's own party rose in Parliament to condemn the army that had taken Rome just two days previously as "slackers, stay-behinds and D-Day Dodgers."

The long-range winter patrols in the Apennines in the winter of 1943-44, crossing the spine of Italy that formed a gap between the Fifth and Eighth armies, were real, though relatively few of them were made by forces as large as a platoon, and most of them were made by Free French and British Commonwealth forces. It was not uncommon for such patrols to have along an officer or two from other Allied nations.

Except for a few survivors' accounts, it is hard to imagine how bad it must have been. If you have done ski-packing and mountain-climbing, you might begin by imagining doing both at the same time, mostly at night, for up to two weeks, without ever being able to have a fire, let alone a hot meal, carrying equipment that weighed two or three times what a modern backpacker would take.

Several intact companies and platoons were detached from the Thirty-sixth Infantry Division after the disaster at the Rapido, but as far as I have been able to find out, none of them were sent out on the Apennine patrols. The Second Platoon depicted in this book is entirely my invention.

The question of why the Nazis, who stopped at so little, declined to use sarin and its chemical cousin tabun is still a matter of hot dispute among historians. Some say it was fear that the Allies must have the same weapon, and that retaliation would be harder on Germany; some that Hitler, a gas victim in World War I, was repulsed by the idea; and some that the grotesque, corrupt bureaucracy that was the Third Reich simply did not call these weapons to anyone's attention. In any case, they were not used, and though they might have prolonged the war until American nuclear weapons turned the tide, they probably could not have changed its ultimate outcome.

For the rest of it—this is, of course, an adventure story, and like every story, it's a lie. I have stuck close to facts where they helped, and done my best to cover my tracks where they didn't.

I must acknowledge the special help of two people in my preparation of this book:

Mr. Ashley Grayson, my agent, who, at a time when my life was going very badly, found me what I desperately needed—a project I could do for both fun and profit—with commendable speed, and who put up with all the normal bad behavior of his client, plus the effects of stress and despair, with far more kindness and patience than I deserved.

And Mr. John D. Barnes, an invaluable source of information for the sort of things that are almost impossible to find in a history book, who served with the First Marine Division in the Korean War, using the same equipment, in similar conditions, in a war just as forgotten. Whatever accuracy or verisimilitude you find here, he had a hand in. Any errors or lapses can be blamed entirely on me, for my negligent failure to ask Dad.

A BID FOR ULTIMATE POWER PITS NOMAD AGAINST A RUTHLESS TECHNOMESSIAH.

NOMAD

DAVID ALEXANDER

Code Name: Nomad—an elite operative trained to fight the ultimate technological war game. Waging high-stakes battles against technoterrorism, Nomad is a new breed of commando.

The year is 2030. The battle is over satellite-harnessed energy. The enemy is the supercomputer controlling the satellite network. This time, the game is real—and the prize is life on earth.
